"You don't have to spell it out. Now take your hands off me."

A murderous gleam came into Al's eyes, but he realized she was goading him and said with silky venom, "Do take the tape and the photos with you when you go—I've got plenty more copies."

"No thanks." Kenzie strode to the door, paused and looked back. "I hope you thought carefully before you decided to start this vendetta...because my job gives me a great deal of power—and I fully intend to use it!"

"I didn't expect anything else."

It was becoming harder by the minute to keep up the act. Kenzie knew that she had to get out or she would break down in front of him. And there was nothing now to say, so she merely gave him one last cold look, nodded and walked away.

SALLY WENTWORTH began her publishing career at a Fleet Street newspaper in London, where she thrived in the hectic atmosphere. After her marriage, she and her husband moved to rural Hertfordshire, where Sally had been raised. There is always a novel on her bedside table, and she also enjoys crafts, plays bridge and attends the ballet and theater regularly.

Books by Sally Wentworth

SALLY WENTWORTH

Practise to Deceive

Harlequin Books

TORONTO • NEW YORK • LONDON
AMSTERDAM • PARIS • SYDNEY • HAMBURG
STOCKHOLM • ATHENS • TOKYO • MILAN
MADRID • WARSAW • BUDAPEST • AUCKLAND

ISBN 0-373-11701-9

PRACTISE TO DECEIVE

Copyright © 1993 by Sally Wentworth.

All rights reserved. Except for use in any review, the reproduction or utilization of this work in whole or in part in any form by any electronic, mechanical or other means, now known or hereafter invented, including xerography, photocopying and recording, or in any information storage or retrieval system, is forbidden without the written permission of the publisher, Harlequin Enterprises Limited, 225 Duncan Mill Road, Don Mills, Ontario, Canada M3B 3K9.

All characters in this book have no existence outside the imagination of the author and have no relation whatsoever to anyone bearing the same name or names. They are not even distantly inspired by any individual known or unknown to the author, and all incidents are pure invention.

This edition published by arrangement with Harlequin Enterprises B.V.

® and TM are trademarks of the publisher. Trademarks indicated with ® are registered in the United States Patent and Trademark Office, the Canadian Trade Marks Office and in other countries.

Printed in U.S.A.

CHAPTER ONE

IT WAS time to move in for the kill. Kenzie continued to smile appreciatively at the man she was interviewing, to nod as if she completely agreed with what he was saying, but she was merely waiting for the right moment now. He could see the clock on the studio wall and knew that there was little time left, so he was becoming complacent, sure in his own mind that he was one of her 'saints' rather than a 'sinner'. Although he had tried not to show it, he had been sweating with nervousness at first, his fat face shiny with it, wishing himself anywhere but there. But such was Donna Mackenzie's reputation and popularity with the public that when she rang and asked to do an interview there were few who dared refuse.

He paused and she said, her voice as sweet as honey, 'It sounds as if the children entrusted into your care at the school have the best of attention.'

'Yes, indeed,' he agreed heartily.

Leaning forwards, her voice sharpening, Kenzie thrust in the sword. 'But the children at the school you ran in north London only five years ago received a little too much of your attention, didn't they, Mr Robins? Or should I say Winterson—that was the name you were using when you were convicted for child abuse, wasn't it? A fact that you conveniently forgot to tell the governors of your current school when you were appointed to the post.'

Her victim tried to bluff it out, to bluster that she'd made a mistake, but her strength was in never getting her facts wrong, and the television audience knew it. He knew it, too; his face had gone deathly pale and his hands were trembling.

'It was easy to drop your surname and use your second name instead, wasn't it?' Kenzie pressed home. 'And the governors were so short-staffed they were glad to employ anyone—anyone who said they'd been working as a headmaster abroad and had such glowing references, references that unfortunately couldn't be properly checked because the country had been torn apart by a civil war.'

The man tried to get up from his chair, to escape, but she was ready for that one and quickly got to her feet and stood over him, preventing him from rising unless he pushed her bodily out of the way. Instead he gripped the arms of his chair, staring up at her in dread, as if she was some dark fate come to crucify him, which in a way she was.

'Oh, the governors were gullible,' she went on, her green eyes fixed on his face, 'but you were so persuasive, so full of innovative ideas for improving the school, that they looked on you as a godsend. They watched you at first, but you managed to behave yourself and lived up to all their hopes, so they trusted you and left you alone.' Lifting her arm in a sudden, dramatic gesture, Kenzie pointed her finger at him. 'How many times have you betrayed that trust? How many children have suffered because of your perversions?' Switching to face the audience, her red hair swirling about her head, Kenzie said forcefully, 'A child this man abused in the past happened to see him and came to me. Hopefully we've been able to prevent Winterson doing too much harm at the new school. But I want you to look at him, ladies and gentlemen. Take a good look at his face. And if you are the governor of a school or have anything to do with children, and he comes to you for a job, don't let him anywhere near them.'

It would have been difficult for the audience to have seen Winterson's face at that moment because he had buried it in his hands and his shoulders were shaking, but the message had got across. The camera panned back to her and Kenzie's face lost its former hardness. 'That's it for tonight, ladies and gentlemen. I'm taking a break for a couple of months but then I'll be back with another live interview, so why don't you join me then and find out whether the person I'll be interviewing will be a ''saint'' or a ''sinner''?'

She stood there, smiling, listening to the applause from the audience, a spontaneous applause that owed nothing to any floor manager's instruction board. Then the signature tune and the logo *Saints or Sinners* replaced her face on the screen and Kenzie was able to relax. Somebody had whisked her latest victim away while he was still in shock, before he could get belligerent and nasty, which they sometimes did. Although it was amazing, really, how calmly some people took it, as if, after her first accusation, there was no point in putting up a fight.

The audience, though, both in the studio and in their homes, preferred it the other way, when the victims tried to argue and shout, to get angry and hurl abuse at her. They liked it when she got tough in return, making irrefutable accusations, tearing reputations to shreds, using her voice and her face to express the loathing that she—and by implication the whole audience—must feel towards the person she was exposing. Several times she had been physically attacked, and not only by men, but there was always a broad-shouldered bodyguard on hand to protect her.

Kenzie had no illusions about her audience; she thought of them as similar to the Roman hordes who had gone to the arenas to watch the gladiators fight, breathlessly waiting for someone to be torn to pieces. That she interviewed almost as many people that she classified as saints didn't seem to make any difference; she knew that it was the sinners they were all waiting to see. Now she thanked the studio audience, the anonymous rows of faces who somehow all seemed to have the same face: eyes agog, excited and satisfied, pleased with the sacrifice that had been thrown to them, their mouths open, showing their teeth as they smiled and clapped her again.

A sudden wave of revulsion filled her, so great that Kenzie had to quickly turn away in case the audience saw and guessed what she was thinking. As she did so she noticed a man who had been sitting near the back stand up to leave. He was tall, she noted, and well dressed in a dark business suit, not the type who usually came to watch the show. Her eyes went to his face, but she caught only a glimpse of a clean-cut jawline before the man turned away and went quickly out of the door at the back of the tiers of seats. Briefly she wondered who he was, whether he was one of the executives from the television company, or a possible sponsor. He certainly didn't look as if he'd applied for a ticket to watch the show and waited the two or three months it took to get to the top of the waiting-list.

'Marvellous! As always, Donna, darling.' The producer came up to congratulate her. He had reason to be grateful: the show, although short, was one of the most popular on television, with a viewing audience of millions, and had made his reputation as well as enhancing Kenzie's. She, though, had already made a name for herself on radio and local television before making it to the national network.

She nodded, feeling suddenly deathly tired as she always did at the end of a show, as she'd done years ago as an actress after a performance. Not that there was much difference, really; it was still all an act. 'Thanks. It seemed to go well.'

She carefully didn't ask what had happened to Winterson; it was a rule she'd had to make for herself or she would never have been able to go on with it. She deliberately didn't even think about the people she'd exposed, only that she'd been right to do it, that they deserved all that they'd got.

'We've got several more people lined up for when you get back. There's a——'

But Kenzie held up her hand to stop him. 'Keep it till then, OK?'

The producer laughed. 'OK. Are you looking forward to your holiday?'

'Definitely,' Kenzie answered, with such feeling that he laughed again.

'Where are you going?'

But that was a secret she wasn't about to divulge to anyone, especially the producer, who was quite capable of intruding into her well-earned break. So Kenzie merely smiled and said, 'To America, to stay with some friends who live near Las Vegas.'

'Sounds glitzy,' he remarked without envy.

'Oh, definitely. I'm going to go to all the shows and break the bank in every casino,' she said flippantly. 'See you in a couple of months' time.' Kenzie made a farewell gesture and walked towards her dressing-room, grinning inwardly; the destination she'd given him had been as far away from the truth as she could get. The bodyguard walked beside her, his eyes watchful, saw her into the room, which had an unmarked door, and listened for the lock to turn before he went away.

Babs, her secretary, was waiting in the dressing-room. 'Another good programme, Donna.'

'You watched it?'

'Yes, upstairs.' She gestured towards a small table that Kenzie used as a desk. 'I'm afraid there's a pile of letters for you to sign.'

'OK, I'll do them after I change. And you needn't bother to wait; I'll put them in the envelopes and post them. I'm sure you're as eager to get away as I am.'

'I'll say. Two weeks of soaking up the sun in Spain; I can't wait.'

Kenzie took off the suit she'd been wearing, the skirt straight and taut across the hips, the jacket quite low cut where it buttoned at the front. Under it she'd worn only a bra, no blouse, sex appeal being part of the package she gave the public. She had no illusions about that, either. The viewers liked to see such an attractive young woman, first soft and beguiling, then turning into a tigress. 'The Tiger Lady', she knew, was one of the names used to describe her in the media. At other times she'd been called a she-devil and a preying mantis—the latter deliberately misspelt. But it was all publicity, all adding to the image she had deliberately set out to create.

Sitting down at the dressing-table with its circle of bright electric bulbs, Kenzie started to cream off her make-up. Babs was in a chatty mood, telling her about some of the letters, although they both knew that Kenzie would go through them with meticulous care before she signed them, as she had already gone through the original letters. Most of these were just from fans asking for photos and autographs, of course; others were bitchy missives from people who wanted her to expose an enemy or even a neighbour they'd fallen out with, sometimes for the flimsiest of reasons. But some of them were a genuine cry for help or told of corruption and brutality that they were powerless to stop but knew that Donna Mackenzie had the power to do so. These were carefully gone into, sometimes arranging a meeting with the complainant; at the back of her mind there was always the dreadful fear that someone might try to set her up and then expose *her*. So far that hadn't happened, but in the year that the show had been on Kenzie had made an awful lot of enemies. That fact had been forced on her a great many times, too, in threatening letters and nasty things that had arrived through the post.

The compensation for it all, of course, was in the many absolutely marvellous letters that recommended the 'saints' that she interviewed—letters that told of lives sacrificed to the unselfish care of others, of unsung doctors and nurses who gave unstintingly of their time, and of neighbours who cared for the old when their own relatives had abandoned them. Sometimes, when she interviewed these people, Kenzie had to take them completely by surprise, because they were far too modest to want any acclaim for what they did. Then her job was a joy and she would go home happy. Not like tonight. Tonight had been another destruction job.

'Oh, and there's a man who wants to see you,' Babs added, consulting her notes. 'He didn't give his name but he said it was in connection with the Clive Ellison programme.'

Kenzie frowned. 'That was ages ago, wasn't it?'

'Over six months. But the man said he had some new information.'

'Well, it's too late now. Ring down to Reception and tell him I'm sorry but I can't see him. Ask him to write in, and if it's of any importance we'll look into it when I get back from holiday.'

Babs nodded and picked up the phone. 'Hello, I think you've got a man there who's waiting to see Donna Mackenzie. Yes. Will you tell him that——? Oh!' Her voice sharpened with surprise. 'Yes, I dare say, but the receptionist would have given you the message. No, this is her secretary. Speak to her yourself?' Babs raised an eyebrow at Kenzie, who shook her head vehemently and pointed at the door. 'No, I'm sorry, sir,' Babs said smoothly. 'I'm afraid Miss Mackenzie has already left.' She listened for a moment. 'You didn't see her because she left by a side-entrance. But if you write to her and let her have this information about Clive Ellison I assure you that she will most certainly look into it and——' She stopped, then shrugged. 'He hung up. Well, it can't have been that important or he would have got in touch long before now.'

'Maybe I should have seen him,' Kenzie said with a troubled frown.

'You can't see everyone who comes to the studios,' Babs protested.

'No, but maybe this was the one I should have seen. Ring back and tell him that if he doesn't mind waiting I'll see him when I leave.'

Babs did so, but shook her head. 'He's gone.' She straightened up. 'And I'm off, too. Have a good holiday, Donna.'

'And you. Have a great time.'

When she'd gone Kenzie finished cleaning her face, then lifted her hands to take off the wig of long auburn hair. It was part of her image, that wig; it went with the green eyes and biting manner, the reputation for not suffering fools gladly, and cheats and rogues not at all. Picking up her hairbrush, she brushed out her own dark hair, which fell in a thick, glistening bob to her neck, then put on a shirt and a pair of jeans. Now she was no longer Donna Mackenzie, television personality, just Mackenzie Heydon, failed actress, the side of her life that she kept very private and as secret as possible.

For another hour she sat and went through the letters, then put them in the envelopes ready to post. Really tired now, Kenzie glanced at her watch; it was almost ten, time for the audience for a recorded quiz show to leave. Gathering up her things, Kenzie perched a pair of tinted glasses on her nose and slipped out of the dressing-room and down the corridor to where the first of the audience were emerging. She mingled with them, just another spectator in her casual clothes, almost unrecognisable from the avenging television star of two hours ago, and went out with them through the heavy glass doors into the street outside.

Kenzie had reason to be grateful for her change of image; not only did it safeguard her privacy, but it had also saved her from harm more than once, when people she had exposed had waited outside to try to attack her, too angry to care about the consequences. Tonight there was no one waiting, although she did notice a man sitting in a car not far away, his gaze fixed on the entrance. But she dismissed it at once; just somebody waiting for his date, probably, or a chauffeur waiting for his boss; there were several well-known people who'd taken part in the quiz show.

Situated in the heart of London's West End, the street was busy, as it always was at this time on Friday nights. They were young people, mostly, up for a good time,

but soon the theatres would be emptying and there would
be older people in smart dresses and suits instead of the
denims of the young. Kenzie found a post-box and
pushed the pile of letters through the slot. She could
have left them with the receptionist to post, but that
would have singled her out from the crowd. And she
had to be careful; the security people at the studios were
always trying to impress that on her. Kenzie took more
notice of their admonitions now; at first she'd taken it
all lightly, confident it couldn't happen to her. But once,
when she'd been making a public appearance as Donna
Mackenzie, one of the 'sinners' from a previous programme had tried to throw acid in her face. He'd been
so nervous that his aim had been erratic, and the bodyguard had been on the alert and had put up his hand in
front of her face. But it had badly shaken Kenzie, and
had left the guard with a scarred hand. So now she
listened.

Walking down the road, she caught a tube at Leicester
Square station and rode the few stops to where she lived
in a modest flat in a house situated in north London, a
place so unpretentious that no one would have dreamed
of her living there. It was noisy; there was a music school
near by and several of the students lodged at the house.
Often they felt the need to sing or play far into the night,
driving out those who wouldn't or couldn't tolerate it.
But Kenzie didn't mind; in fact she rather enjoyed lying
in bed and listening to the sound of the jazz group that
practised in the basement or being lulled to sleep by a
violin solo from the flat above.

The violin was playing tonight and her bed looked very
inviting, but the night wasn't over yet. Kenzie went to
the small kitchen area and made herself a cup of coffee
which she drank while she waited. At eleven-fifteen a

knock came at the door and she opened it to a very tough-looking young black man. He grinned at her. 'Ready?'

Kenzie nodded, put her jacket back on, and joined him outside. They walked down the dark street together, past littered gutters and pavements where the open market had been, past pubs that had just closed, the drinkers still standing around outside, reluctant to go home, raucous and belligerent. Some of the drinkers made comments as they passed, but her companion was too big and menacing for them to try anything. They reached their destination, an ordinary-looking house in an ordinary road, and went inside, greeting the people who were already there. Kenzie took off her jacket and sat down at a table, and adjusted the angle-poise light so that it shone on the pad of paper and the telephone. Within minutes a call came through and she answered it, her voice warm, encouraging. 'Hello. This is Friends in Need, and my name's Kenzie. How can I help you?'

Usually a night shift was exactly that—it lasted all night, from ten p.m. until eight o'clock the next morning. Today, however, Kenzie was helping to fill in for another volunteer who had been taken ill recently, sharing the shift with someone else, so she worked for only five hours. But those hours were some of the busiest of the whole day—the small hours of the morning when troubled people couldn't sleep, when the other side of the bed was empty and life was so lonely that it seemed pointless to go on living. It was then, when they were at their most vulnerable, that people picked up a phone and dialled the number, sure of a sympathetic voice at the other end of the line.

At five in the morning, Kenzie's replacement arrived, again escorted by Winston, the black youth whom they had once helped and who had designated himself as their night-time minder. He walked Kenzie home and she tumbled into bed, falling immediately asleep.

There was a telephone and a fax-machine at the flat, both numbers known to very few people. When the alarm went off at nine-thirty, Kenzie found a message on the fax, relayed from her office at the television studios. 'Caller wishes you to contact this number *re* the Ellison case. Says is urgent.'

Kenzie read the message while she was pulling on her clothes. Her cases were packed and, because of her late night, she'd left getting up until the last possible moment. She rushed around, putting last-minute things into a flight bag, then decided to forgo her morning glass of orange juice so that she could make the call. She rang the number, and got a crossed line. She tried again, but this time the line was busy. Throwing down the receiver in annoyance, Kenzie made sure the water and gas were turned off, that the fridge was empty, that she'd got her ticket and passport. Picking up the phone again, she pressed the redial button. This time it began to ring. Almost immediately, though, there was a loud honking outside and she knew her taxi had arrived. At the same time the saxophonist in the next-door flat began to rehearse. Giving up, Kenzie started to put down the receiver when a woman's voice said the number. The taxi hooted again. Kenzie hesitated then put down the phone; she would have to shout above the noise, the call would probably be long and involved, and time was getting short; she didn't want to lose the taxi or miss the plane. She flipped on the answerphone then yelled out of the window that she was on her way.

Less than eight hours later Kenzie was eagerly looking out of the window of the taxi that she'd picked up at

Faro airport, searching for the first glimpse of the villa. It was the moment she always looked forward to most, her heart full of excitement. The road, narrow and pot-holed, climbed a steep hill, then straightened out along the ridge, and there it was: an old, pantiled roof, mellow with time, just showing through the trees in the valley below. Kenzie let out a long sigh of both satisfaction and anticipation. Home at last. For this small house tucked into the fold of the hills was home to her as the flat in London had never been. Here she could forget London, work, her *alter ego*—especially the latter—and just be herself. For eight whole wonderful, glorious weeks!

The taxi driver dumped her and her luggage in the little courtyard in front of the house and drove away in a cloud of dust, the noise of his engine straining as it climbed back up the hill. Kenzie waited until the sound had faded completely and the only noises were those of bees buzzing in the sunflowers that grew against the wall, and the faint click of cicadas in the long grass of the field behind the house. Only then did she go up to the wooden door, unlock it, and walk into the cool hall, the last of the evening sunlight laying a path for her.

The place was clean and neat, flowers in vases in every room, and the garden, too, was well-tended. Maria and Antonio had, as always, looked after the place well in her absence. For a while Kenzie just wandered around the garden, feeling less tense by the minute, the peace of her surroundings acting like a strong tranquilliser. When it grew dark she went inside, switched on the lamps, and took her case upstairs to unpack. She hadn't brought many clothes with her—she kept enough here for her needs—but there were presents for Maria and Antonio and their family, who all lived in the village a mile or so away. And there were things she'd made or bought for the villa: a Victorian counterpane for the spare bedroom, a picture she'd embroidered in tiny stitches and some new towels for the bathroom.

When she'd unpacked she went down to the kitchen to make herself a coffee and found an envelope stuck on the fridge door, marked, 'To the owner'. Inside was a letter from the young couple to whom she had lent the villa for a few weeks. The wife had rung Friends in Need and Kenzie had answered; between sobs of despair she'd told her story. Her husband was a junior doctor, working in a hospital, often for seventy or eighty hours a week, for very little money. She'd had to give up her job to look after their two-year-old twins, and now they were faced with eviction from their flat because the rent had been put up. She was tired to death and deeply depressed, on the edge of a breakdown.

Kenzie had let her talk herself out, soothed and comforted. Friends in Need were supposed to play a passive role, but there were times when Kenzie felt that a little active—but always anonymous—help was called for. The woman had used her husband's Christian name and the name of the hospital, so it had been easy to trace them. The doctor had been told that an all-expenses-paid holiday had been donated to the hospital and he was to be the recipient. Then a lonely old lady, another caller, had offered them the use of half her large house and garden for a nominal rent, if the couple would keep an eye on her.

The letter was full of thanks, and, what was even more gratifying, full of optimism for the future.

I'm afraid the kids broke a vase, but we've replaced it, plus another to make a pair. Hope you like them.

Again, whoever you are, thank you, thank you, thank you.

Kenzie smiled, found the vases, which were full of flowers, and decided she did like them. They weren't her first 'guests' by any means, and Maria and Antonio were used by now to not divulging her name, always referring to her as the *senhorita*. They tended to look on it as a sort of game, but were always as kind and welcoming to the people to whom she lent the villa as they were to Kenzie.

It took Kenzie a couple of weeks to really wind down, to put England and work completely out of her mind, to settle into the pace of that quiet Portuguese backwater. There was a small pool in the garden, and she spent a lot of time swimming and sunbathing, often falling asleep and waking feeling sated by the sun. It was always like this: she worked herself to a standstill and had to come here to recover. To find herself again. To fall asleep like a child whenever she was tired, eat when she was hungry, and put all responsibilities out of her mind. She'd had the villa for four years now, had seen it when she'd come to Portugal on holiday and had hired a bicycle to take a trip inland. She'd got a puncture and had wheeled the bicycle off the road and down this track to get help. The house had been empty, its owner having gone to live with her daughter, and within a very short time Kenzie had managed to buy it. Her career, or rather her *new* career, had only just been starting to take off then, and it had taken all the money she had had, but Kenzie had never for a moment regretted it. As she had prospered, so had she improved the villa, having electricity and drainage connected, and putting in bathrooms and the pool. But she was always careful not to

overdo it, to keep the intrinsic nature of the house that
had first attracted her.

One of the biggest assets was that the villa wasn't
overlooked, so she could wear a modicum of clothes as
she sunbathed or worked in the garden. Her skin soon
became tanned, except for a white strip across her hips,
and when she strolled down to the village to shop she
looked almost as brown as the olive-skinned people she
met. All the food she needed Kenzie was able to buy in
the village or from the neighbouring farms, but after
she'd been at the villa for three weeks or so she got out
the bicycle she kept there and rode the few miles into
the nearest town.

The town seemed to get busier every time Kenzie came
to Portugal; it was about a mile from the coast and separated from it by the main road that ran all along the
Algarve, parallel to the sea. On the other side of the
road there had once been a small fishing village, but
now there were rows of modern villas climbing the hills
to either side, with golf courses and apartment blocks
on the outskirts. Supermarkets had replaced the little
one-roomed shops in the fishing village, but a great many
of the visitors came to the town to use the banks and to
buy furniture and equipment for their holiday homes.
So the town was prospering, with several new shops, and
the pavement cafés in the square were kept busy, the
customers sitting under splendid new sun umbrellas,
Kenzie noticed.

Kenzie propped her bike against the wall outside the
wine store, where she ordered a couple of cases of *vinho
verde* to be sent out to the villa. She was an old customer
so had to be properly welcomed, and the store owner's
family had to be asked after in her ever improving
Portuguese. She was given some port to taste and a

present of a packet of sweets. It was all so friendly, so leisurely, so different from London. After the wine store there was the post office, the fish stall at the daily market before it closed, and then some lunch at a table outside one of the cafés.

It was quite busy, in a good position near the post office and the two banks in the town. Quite a lot of locals were eating there, but Kenzie wasn't at all surprised to see several visitors, too, their paler skins and holiday clothes setting them apart. Some of them were reading English-language newspapers that they'd bought, but Kenzie carefully kept her eyes away from the headlines; she didn't want to know a thing until she had to go back. There was a man sitting near the front of the café with a paper, although he didn't seem to be reading it; his eyes kept going round the square as if he was looking for someone. A wife or girlfriend, probably, Kenzie guessed; he was certainly good-looking enough not to be alone.

Sitting down at a free table, Kenzie felt his eyes flick over her, but then the man resumed his search of the square. The waiter was new; he didn't recognise her. Kenzie gave her order in Portuguese, and asked him to pass on her compliments to the proprietor, who was another old friend. The waiter gave a rather harassed nod and hurried away. He brought her drink, getting his priorities right, and Kenzie settled down to one of her favourite pastimes—people-watching. From a very early age she had wanted to be an actress and her first drama teacher, recognising her enthusiasm, had taught her how to look at people and observe their mannerisms, the way they moved and gestured. It had become a habit, even though her acting now consisted of just one part. But it was still fun to look at someone and imagine herself inside their skin.

There was a couple sitting not far away, the woman young, blonde and shapely, the man older, his hair greying. A second marriage for him, Kenzie guessed, and could imagine the whole scenario of the older man abandoning a wife of long standing to marry his mistress. The woman was leaning towards him, talking persuasively, touching him a lot. He was shaking his head, but the woman kept on, as a child did if it wanted something, until the man suddenly threw up his hands in a gesture of surrender and nodded. The woman smiled then, pleased, content, and kissed him enthusiastically. The man took his wallet from his pocket and passed over some money, which the woman took, and then she hurried away, her high heels clicking on the pavement.

Kenzie had enjoyed the little scene, but the woman had been too much of a clichéd character to be really interesting. Letting her eyes move on, Kenzie came to the man with the paper again. He turned a page, folding it carefully. A meticulous man, she thought. But again, instead of reading it, he seemed to be looking over the top of the paper at the people in the square. He was a tall man, his legs stretched out before him under the table, and his shoulders were broad. He had dark hair, thick, and long enough to be lifted by the slight breeze that blew off the sea. Only able to see him in profile from where she was sitting, to the right and slightly behind him, Kenzie saw a lean face with straight brow and good bone-structure, the jawline very firm. About thirty, she guessed, and he looked very self-assured, very fit.

Suddenly he tensed. Following his eyes as he looked across the square, Kenzie saw that a car had pulled up and a woman was getting out of it, obviously a holiday-maker as she had reddish hair and white skin. The woman turned to supervise some children who had followed her out of the car. She was about forty, rather short and dumpy. Looking back at the man, Kenzie saw him relax again and lift his glass to drink. Not the person he was waiting for, then.

Kenzie began to be intrigued by him, but her food arrived, and then her attention was caught by three girls who came to the café, clearly in the middle of an argument, so she watched them while she ate. When she'd finished she ordered a coffee, and reminded the waiter of her message to the proprietor. Two minutes later the owner came hurrying out, arms lifted in an expansive gesture of welcome. 'Senhorita Mackenzie! Such a pleasure to see you again.'

He spoke quite loudly and several heads turned to look, among them the man with the paper, who swung round in his seat.

Kenzie smilingly stood to shake hands and greet him, to ask after the proprietor's family.

'They are all very well. Please, you will come into the café when you have finished? My wife and daughters, they will be pleased to see you again. Often they speak of the Senhorita Mackenzie.'

Kenzie promised and sat down to drink her coffee, which was accompanied by a large cake, with the compliments of the owner. At leisure to look round again, she saw the three girls were sulking and not speaking to each other, and the man with the paper must have seen whoever he was waiting for, because he had finished his drink and was leaving some money on the table to pay his bill. Putting on a pair of sunglasses, he walked quickly off to the right and out of sight. For a brief instant, as he walked away, he seemed vaguely familiar, but then Kenzie shrugged, sure that she'd never seen him before. She felt a slight feeling of disappointment at not seeing who he'd been waiting for, but quickly forgot him as the woman she'd seen originally rejoined her husband. Sitting next to him, she took out a ring box, opened it, and put the gold ring inside on *his* finger. So she'd wanted the money to spend on him! How wrong could you get? Kenzie thought with a smile. It just proved that you should never jump to conclusions. Her meal finished, she went back into the café to see the proprietor's family and spend some time chatting to them.

By the time she came out it was three o'clock and the bank was open again. It was busy, as always in holiday time, with a queue of people waiting to change money and traveller's cheques. Kenzie patiently waited her turn, then walked back to her bicycle, loading all her purchases into its ample basket on the front. She began to pedal back towards the villa, keeping to the side as cars and trucks went past her in a swirl of dust. On the outskirts of the town a car overtook her, then pulled up a short distance ahead. Kenzie glanced over her shoulder to make sure nothing was coming when she went to go past it, but there was less traffic here. She moved out into the middle of the road to overtake the car, but just as she went to pass the driver's door it suddenly opened forcefully, banging hard against her. Kenzie tried desperately to keep control, but her basket was too heavy. She wobbled dangerously, and the next moment went sprawling in the road.

She ended up with her legs caught in the frame of the bike, her shopping spread in an untidy mess around her. Dazed, and considerably angry, Kenzie lifted herself up on one elbow, aware of a painful leg and arm where they had hit the rough surface of the road. She opened her mouth to yell at the man getting out of the car, but then became aware of the noise of an engine getting very close. Looking up the road, she saw that there was a steep rise, and just coming over it towards where she lay was a large truck, going fast. In sudden terror, she tried to disentangle herself and get up, but her leg was caught in the chain. The truck came thundering nearer, apparently unaware, and Kenzie gave a cry of terror. But the next moment both she and the bicycle had been picked up off the road, and were held in a powerful grip as the truck raced by, flattening her fish, which still lay near where her head had been.

Kenzie gave a great sob of relief and sagged against her rescuer, her legs feeling suddenly weak. He helped her to disentangle herself and stand up, but by then Kenzie had recalled that it was his fault that she had been in danger in the first place. Her fury returning, she pushed away his supporting arm and yelled, 'Why the hell don't you make sure there's no one passing before you open your door?' But then she realised she'd spoken in English and he wouldn't understand. She tried to find the words in Portuguese, but then looked at his face and realised she didn't have to. The man who had knocked her down was the man from the café, the man who'd been pretending to read the paper.

CHAPTER TWO

THERE was sharp concern in the man's voice as he said, 'Are you all right?'

Taken aback by surprise, Kenzie stood staring at him for a moment, but then she became aware of her arm and leg hurting and snapped, 'No, I'm not all right! Why can't you look what you're doing? I could have been killed by that truck.'

'I'm most fearfully sorry. It was entirely my fault. You must be feeling terrible. Why don't you come and sit over here for a minute?'

He led her over to a low wall beside the road, Kenzie limping a little, and helped her to sit down. She opened her mouth to have another go at him, but saw that he looked rather white and shaken himself. Knowing that you'd nearly got someone killed must be almost as big a shock as being the potential victim, she realised.

'I'm so sorry,' he repeated. 'It was a diabolically stupid thing to do. Here, let me look at your leg.'

He squatted in front of her and took hold of her ankle, his touch gentle. He was right, Kenzie thought, it was an abysmally stupid thing to have done, and somehow not something she would have expected of him. But that was silly, too; apart from sitting near him in the same café for half a hour, she didn't know a thing about the man. For all she knew, he could be habitually clumsy and inept.

'Ouch!' She winced as he touched a tender part of her leg and leaned down to look, her face twisting into a grimace as she saw the long graze on her calf. Her elbow, too, was grazed and bloody.

'Those will need cleaning up. I've got a first-aid kit in the car.'

He straightened and went to the car, returning with a small but compact box of bandages and things.

'How lucky—or do you find it necessary to always carry a first-aid kit around with you?' Kenzie asked with irony as he squatted down again.

The man's eyes flicked up at her, aware of her sarcasm. Unusual eyes of a very deep, almost violet blue, she noticed. 'It came with the car,' he said shortly. 'Hold still while I put some antiseptic on it. I'm afraid it might hurt a little when I get the dirt out.'

It did. More than a little. Kenzie's eyes watered, but she blinked rapidly and bit her lip. 'It's—it's not your car, then?' she said, to try to take her mind off the pain.

'No, I hired it.' He finished with her leg and sat astride the wall so that he could work on her arm. She swayed a little as he got busy with the antiseptic again, and he put his hand on her shoulder to steady her. 'Are you all right? Not feeling faint?'

She blinked again. 'No. No, I—I'm fine.'

'Look, I really am most frightfully sorry, Mrs...Miss...?'

'Heydon,' Kenzie managed.

His eyebrows drew into a frown. 'Heydon?'

But her head began to swim and he put his arm round her, holding her against his shoulder for a couple of minutes. Then she straightened up. 'Sorry. The—the shock must have got to me.' She glanced at him and found that he was looking at her face, his eyes intent, searching almost. But when his glance met hers he quickly looked away.

'This won't take more than a minute.' He finished cleaning her arm with deft efficiency, making her wonder if he was a doctor. 'There. Now will you be OK here for a minute while I pick up your shopping?'

Kenzie nodded, and was glad of the few minutes in which to recover a little. Of all the stupid things to happen. As he'd said, it was his fault entirely, but it was also entirely due to him that Kenzie's head hadn't ended up as squashed as her fish. So her emotions towards this stranger were very mixed, both angry and grateful at the same time. He put her shopping back in the basket and wheeled the bike over from round the other side of the car, but it wouldn't wheel properly—the chain was off and the front wheel buckled. Kenzie looked at the latter in confusion; she hadn't realised it was so bent—she didn't think the truck had hit it.

Opening the boot of his car, the man began to lift in the bike, but Kenzie called out, 'Hey, what are you doing?'

'I'm afraid it can't be ridden. I'll take you home.'

'But you can't!'

'No?' He lifted an eyebrow questioningly.

Kenzie lifted her hand to her head in some confusion. 'I—I mean you can't...I don't know you.'

A slight look of amusement creased the man's lips— thin lips, but the lower fuller than the other.

'Well, that can be remedied.' Coming over, he held out his hand to her. 'I'm Al Rogan. Over here on holiday and staying at an apartment near the golf club. And I'm extremely sorry for knocking you down and would like to make amends in whatever way I can. It seems the least I can do is to take you home. I'm afraid the bike is quite unridable, and even if it were OK I don't think you're up to riding it. Do you?'

Slowly Kenzie shook her head. She looked into his face, studying it, but finding only concern there. His mouth twisted suddenly and he gave a short laugh. 'I know that you must think me an absolute fool, but I do know how to drive; I won't crash the car. Oh, and I'm boringly respectable, by the way.'

Kenzie liked his grin, and very much doubted that he was at all boring. Intuition prompting her to trust him, she smiled in return and shook his hand. His grip was strong, his handshake firm.

'I really am most terribly sorry, you know,' he said with sincerity.

She shrugged. 'It was an accident. Just unfortunate that I happened to be coming along, that's all.'

For a moment he looked surprised. 'That's very— magnanimous of you. Here, let me help you into the car.'

He took her arm and helped her up. Kenzie could have managed alone, but found she rather enjoyed being treated as a helpless and frail female. Even so, she was quite glad to sit in the car and gingerly stretch her leg out in front of her. Darn, the grazes were going to ruin her tan, she thought as she looked at them.

Al Rogan dealt with her bike and shopping and came to sit beside her. 'Would you rather I took you to a hospital so that you can have your wounds properly dealt with?' he offered.

'They're hardly wounds. And you seem to have dealt with them pretty efficiently already. Are you a doctor?'

Al grinned and shook his head. 'No, but I got my first-aid badge as a Boy Scout.' He started the engine and looked at her expectantly. 'Where to, then?'

'Oh, it's straight ahead.' They started off and she frowned a little. 'Didn't you stop to visit someone?'

'Visit someone? Oh, I see what you mean. No, I stopped to look at the map.'

'But you must have been going to get out of the car. Why else would you open the door?'

'I was going to spread the map out on the roof.' He gestured towards the back seat. 'It's a large-scale map and I wanted an overall picture, to decide where to spend the afternoon.'

Glancing over her shoulder, Kenzie saw that there was a large map that looked as if it had been thrown into the car haphazardly, as he would have done when rushing to help her after knocking her off her bike. The faint, niggling doubt at the back of her mind subsided and Kenzie said, 'Take the next left.'

He gave her a surprised glance. 'Inland?' When she nodded in confirmation he said, 'I thought all the holiday-makers stayed near the coast. You are on holiday, I take it?'

'Yes, but I prefer to stay further inland.'

'What's wrong with the coast?'

She smiled slightly. 'Too many tourists—and cars.'

'Ouch! I asked for that one.' The road they had turned on to was far less busy, and he was able to give her a longer look. 'But surely that's where all the life is, isn't it? On the coast?'

'You mean night-life?'

'That and all the other activities. Water sports, golf, tennis.'

'I suppose so, if you're into that kind of thing. I just like to relax and unwind.'

'Sounds as if you must have a stressful job,' Al commented.

He paused, waiting for her to enlighten him, but Kenzie chose not to. Instead she indicated the signpost pointing the way to the village. 'It's the next left.'

'Alegre.' He read the sign aloud and for a brief instant a look of something like ruefulness came into his face.

'You seem surprised,' Kenzie said lightly.

His eyes flicked at her. 'I wouldn't have put you down as staying so far off the beaten track. But perhaps you're with your family, or friends?'

'The entrance to the villa is just coming up on the left. Between the two pillars, where the acacia trees are.'

'I see it.'

Al turned the car in through the gateway, the brick pillars almost hidden beneath an encrustation of lichen and the drooping swaths of the trees, heavy with blossom. There was a sign, 'Villa Mimosa', but that, too, was almost obscured. The driveway meandered downhill, ending in a circle before the house, its centre a fountain with a bronze dolphin that had gone green and didn't play any more. Stopping the car, Al got out and stood staring at the old house, its walls covered in climbing plants—roses, mostly—in yellow, peach and full-blown white. Remembering Kenzie, he came round to help her out.

'What a beautiful place. No wonder you'd rather stay here than in one of the estates near the coast.' Putting a strong hand under her elbow, Al helped her over to the front door.

There was a spare key tucked away on the gable of the porch, and Kenzie would normally have used it to let herself in, but now she took another key from her purse and opened the door with that. 'I think I can manage now, thanks,' she said lightly.

'Of course. I'll get your shopping.'

She waited on the doorstep while he brought the basket from her bicycle. It was a big basket and it was full. Al raised an eyebrow, but Kenzie knew she couldn't manage it. 'If you wouldn't mind carrying it into the kitchen for me?'

'Of course not.'

He followed her into the house, along the stone-flagged floor of the hallway to the kitchen. Kenzie hadn't turned this into a late-twentieth-century dream of fitted cupboards with not a thing out of place, instead keeping it as a country kitchen with the addition of modern amenities. The fireplace was still there, although it didn't get lit very much in the summer, flowers were hanging to dry from the beams, and in the centre of the room was a big wooden table. There were four chairs round the table, and in front of each the things that Kenzie had been amusing herself with as and when she felt like it. In one place there was a sewing frame and a pile of silks and wools, and in another a sketch that she'd done of some flowers and which she was trying to paint over with water-colours. At the third side of the table there were a pile of books on gardening and a notepad, and at the fourth her cassette tapes and *Teach Yourself Portuguese* books.

Al went to put the basket on the table, then grinned when he saw that there wasn't any room. 'You all look very busy.'

'You can put it on here.' Kenzie pointed to a smaller worktable by the sink. When he'd done so she hesitated, not sure what to do or say. A deep-down basic instinct made her want to offer Al a drink, to have him stay so that she could get to know him better. If she had been plain Mackenzie Heydon, over here on holiday, she probably would have done so without even thinking about it. But also having been Donna Mackenzie for quite some years now had made her wary, especially since the *Saints or Sinners* programme had taken off. Too many people had tried to get to know her just because she was a celebrity for her to take any meeting with someone new at face value.

The decision was taken out of her hands. Al said, 'Why don't you sit down and tell me where to put all this stuff?' He pulled a chair round for her and then turned his back as he started to take things out of the basket. 'Have you got a cat?'

Kenzie sat in the chair, wishing that her arm and leg would stop smarting. 'No, but one comes to call every morning.'

'You'd better give him the fish then; I'm afraid it's unfit for human consumption. But the fruit looks OK.' He looked round, saw the fruit bowl in the middle of the table, and loaded it up. 'What about this pâté?'

'There's a fridge behind you.'

He dealt with the rest of the shopping without having to ask, putting the embroidery silks she'd bought with the others on the table, and the washing-up liquid by the sink. 'That seems to be the lot.' Al turned, leaned back against the worktable, and smiled at her. It was a most attractive smile, his eyes crinkling, looking at her with real friendliness. 'Now is there anything else I can do for you to make amends, Miss Heydon? It is "Miss", isn't it?' he added, glancing at her ringless left hand.

'Yes. My bicycle is still in your car,' she reminded him.

'Where it's going to stay until I find a place where they can repair it.' He held up a hand as she opened her mouth. 'And please don't say that it isn't necessary; I insist.'

Kenzie smiled. 'I was going to say that there's a repair shop back in the town. In the street that leads up to the smaller church.'

He laughed, his blue eyes amused. 'Good. I'll take it there straight away. Let's hope they're not too busy. When it's ready shall I phone you and let you know I'm bringing it over?'

'I'm afraid there isn't any phone.'

His eyebrows rising, Al said, 'You really do like to get away from it all, don't you?' He straightened up. 'I'd better get going. Don't bother to see me out.'

But Kenzie went with him anyway. Outside he stopped to look round again. 'This is the most fantastic place. How on earth did you find it?'

'Quite by chance,' Kenzie replied lightly.

Al turned to look at her, his long-lashed eyes quizzical. 'I hope you'll forgive me for what happened.'

'Of course.'

'And will there be an irate boyfriend or relative who'll come gunning for me?'

She laughed and shook her head. 'No. You're quite safe.'

'Good.' He nodded and got into the car, and waved as he pulled away.

Kenzie hadn't encouraged him to linger, but as she watched Al go she wished she'd offered him a drink so that he would have stayed longer. There was a casual attractiveness about him that she rather liked. Because she was in television she met a lot of famous and glamorous people: show-biz personalities, actors, film stars. Most of them were pleasant, genuine people, but they were aware always of their image, of the impression they were making. To meet someone different was always interesting. And she had liked his smile.

Her grazes meant that she couldn't swim that day or the next, which was a nuisance, but apart from that she was fine, not even any nightmares about the truck thundering towards her. Her thoughts, though, did tend to drift towards Al Rogan, but only—she told herself—because she wondered if he was having any difficulty in getting the bike repaired. Lots of people hired bikes in the summer and the repair shops were often busy.

But he was back only two days after the accident, arriving at about four in the afternoon. Kenzie was out in the garden, sunbathing, but heard the car drive up and had time to pull a loose T-shirt over her naked chest.

'Anyone home?' Al was standing near the front door, looking up at the house, hands on his hips.

'Hello.' Kenzie walked round the corner of the house, her hair tied back with a ribbon, her legs long and shapely.

'Hello, again.' Al's eyes went over her, an appreciative and very masculine glint in them as his glance lingered on her legs. 'How are you? No ill effects from when we last ran into one another, I hope?'

Wrinkling her nose at the pun, Kenzie said, 'No, I'm fine, thanks.'

'Your leg certainly looks OK,' he remarked, his eyes heading in that direction again. Then he turned to get her bicycle out of his car. 'Here we are, all in working order again.'

'That was quick. Usually they take at least a week.'

'I used bribery and corruption,' he admitted with a grin. 'They mended the chain and put on a new wheel. Would you like to try it?'

'No, I'm sure it's fine. Thanks.'

'Where shall I put it?'

'It lives in an outhouse, round the back.'

Kenzie led the way and Al put the bike in the little pantiled building that had once been an outside loo, but where she now kept all her gardening tools. He guessed what it was and laughed, then said, 'I have something else for you.'

When he came back he was carrying a cardboard grocery box. 'I got you some fish to replace the other lot. And some wine to drink it down with. I hope you and the rest of your party didn't starve that night?'

'No, of course not. And the cat was grateful.'

He set the box down on the table near the solitary lounger where she'd been sunbathing, then looked round at the pool and the garden. 'This really is the most delightful house. Have you rented it for long? Do you think the owner would let it to me after you leave? If it's vacant, of course.'

'I'm afraid it isn't available for rent; it's a private villa.' Kenzie smiled at him. 'Thank you for the fish. I'd better put it in the fridge.'

She picked up the paper-wrapped parcel and carried it inside, found a plate, and began to unpack it. Inside were about two dozen of the big delicious sardines for which the Algarve was famous. 'Good heavens, what a lot.'

Al followed her as far as the door and leaned on the jamb. 'I wasn't sure how many there were in your party.'

Glancing at him under her lashes, Kenzie hesitated, then impulsively decided to trust him. 'There's just me.' But then caution reasserted itself and she added quickly, 'At the moment.'

'In that case you'll be living off fish for a week—or else the cat will have the time of his life.'

'Perhaps you'd like to take some back?'

'Definitely not.'

'Don't the people you're with like fish?'

'I'm alone, too. Unfortunately the friend I was going to meet here couldn't make it at the last minute.'

'That was a shame. Has it upset your plans very much?' Kenzie came out of the house to get the wine he'd brought. There was a lot of that, too.

'Quite a bit. It was supposed to be a golfing holiday, but it isn't always easy to get someone to play with you. You don't play golf, do you?' he asked hopefully.

'Sorry, no.' Kenzie put the wine in the fridge but kept back one bottle. 'Would you like a drink? Shall we open one of these now?'

He gave her a quick smile. 'Yes, I would. Thanks.'

Kenzie told Al where to find another lounger and he set it up alongside hers, but not too close. He opened the bottle with the efficiency that she'd come to expect and poured the wine, then leant back against his lounger. Today he was wearing a T-shirt and denim shorts, his legs strong and tanned. 'You know,' he remarked, 'you're incredibly lucky to have this place. You say it's private; does it belong to a relation of yours?'

'Sort of,' Kenzie admitted, thinking that her other self was definitely a relation. 'But it's not for sale.'

'I was afraid of that.'

'Where are you staying?'

'In an apartment near the golf course. A two-bedroomed box sandwiched between a whole load of similar boxes,' he said with a grimace. 'But there's a pool and tennis courts, of course.'

'And it's near all the night-life.'

He nodded, but his voice wasn't very enthusiastic when he said, 'Yes, that too.'

'How long are you here for?'

'We took the apartment for two months.' Seeing her surprised look, he explained, 'I've been working abroad for the last two years and have a huge chunk of leave saved up. And my friend, an ex-colleague, was between jobs, so we thought we'd spend a few weeks playing golf. It seemed a very convenient arrangement, but then his employers offered him a terrific package to stay on, so he had to cancel.'

But Kenzie was hardly listening; her mind had latched on to something that really interested her. She said, keeping her voice casual, 'You've been working abroad? Where was that?'

'In Hong Kong mostly. For a merchant bank. Getting ready for the twenty-first century.'

'And you haven't been back to England in all that time?'

'No. My last holiday I took in Australia about a year ago.'

The *Saints or Sinners* programme was only shown in Britain; it was reckoned to be only of national interest and the programme wasn't sold abroad. Al couldn't have seen it in Hong Kong, or Australia, and he had left England before it had started. So he couldn't possibly know who she was or what she did. It was extremely unlikely, anyway, that he would have recognised her, but the doubt had been in the back of her mind. Now it disappeared completely and Kenzie relaxed visibly; she had been too cautious, had let the security people's warnings make her too guarded.

She gave Al a sudden, dazzling smile. 'This is delicious wine.'

'I'm glad you like it. How long are you on holiday for, Miss . . . ? Look, do I have to keep calling you Miss Heydon? It seems very dated.'

'Of course not. My name's Kenzie.'

His eyes settled on her face. 'Kenzie? That's most unusual.'

'It's short for Mackenzie. My parents had a taste for the unusual.'

'It's certainly that.' He continued to look at her for a long moment, but then he blinked and said, 'Had? Does that mean your parents are dead?'

'Yes, they are.' Quickly she changed the subject, not wanting to talk about it, the hurt still painful even after so many years. 'Are you any good at barbecues? I got a local man to build one for me, but it smokes all the time.'

'Let's have a look.'

They got up and strolled over to the other side of the pool where the brick barbecue was built against the garden wall.

'Here, hold this, would you?' Al gave her his glass and knelt to peer underneath it. 'I'm no expert, but I think you probably need more draught coming from underneath. I could only really tell by trying to cook something on it, though.'

'There's all the sardines you brought,' Kenzie offered, using this indirect way of asking him to stay and eat with her. His eyes flicked to her face and she sensed some tension in him. 'That's if you have time, of course,' she added rather stiffly, remembering that when she'd seen him in the town she'd thought he was waiting for some girl.

'Certainly. A great idea. Where do you keep the stuff to light it with?'

She told him and he set to work while Kenzie went inside to prepare a salad. But Al called to her and when she came out the barbecue was smoking again.

'I think it needs to have a couple of bricks knocked out. Will you trust me to do it?'

Kenzie hesitated, nodded, and went inside so that she didn't have to watch as she heard him hammering at the bricks. Ten minutes later there was more hammering and she began to get mental pictures of the whole thing collapsing, but then all was quiet, and when she came out again, unable to resist her curiosity, she found him watching the barbecue as the hickory blocks began to glow. He grinned at her. 'We now have a smokeless zone.'

'Great!' Kenzie came over to admire. Al had a dirt mark on his cheek and his shirt was damp with perspiration. 'You look hot. Why don't you have a swim to cool off?'

He wiped some drops of sweat from his forehead. 'I'd love to. Only thing is I don't have any trunks with me.'

'I think I can lend you some. Just a minute.' She ran into the house and up to the spare bedroom, to the cupboard where she kept things that her various guests had left behind. She was almost sure... Yes, there was a pair of men's trunks in rather gaudy fluorescent stripes of green, red and yellow that someone had forgotten. Running back with them, she laughingly held them out. 'Will these do? I'm sorry about the colour.'

Al glanced at them and took them from her. For a moment she thought there was a grim set to his face, but then he laughed. 'I shall feel like a traffic light. I'll change in the outhouse.' He looked at her. 'Are you coming in?'

'Sure.'

Going up to her bedroom, Kenzie found a one-piece swimsuit in deep red, the legs cut away high on her hips. It covered more but was far sexier than a bikini. Ruefully she looked at the grazes on her arm and leg; well, they just couldn't be helped. When she came down Al was already in the pool, swimming with an easy crawl that denoted the accomplished swimmer.

'I've an idea you're used to a bigger pool,' she remarked when he came to the side.

He stood up, water cascading from his broad shoulders down his chest, plastering his hair to his head. Lifting his hands, Al wiped his eyes. He was almost directly below her. Lifting his head, he let his eyes travel slowly up her body until they met hers. Kenzie watched him, waiting for him to make some comment on her figure, because her figure, she knew, was quite something. But he took her completely by surprise by saying, 'Well, don't just stand there, woman.' And he grabbed her arm and pulled her in.

The next half-hour was pretty hectic as they played a two-man version of water polo, in which Al chased her round the pool, trying to get the ball off her most of the time. Hectic, but great fun. Kenzie scored a goal, but swallowed a lot of water in the process, and came up spluttering but laughing. 'I won! I won!'

'You're a very competitive lady.' Al heaved himself out and stretched down a hand to help Kenzie, hoisting her up easily.

'You must keep very fit,' she remarked. 'I thought businessmen had huge working meals and were tied to their desks the rest of the day.'

'Only if you want to get ulcers or have a heart attack. I used to work out in a gym several times a week.' They had been standing quite close together, but he moved away. 'Let's see how the barbecue is coming along. It should be hot enough to cook the fish now.'

'OK, I'll dry off and get it.'

She changed in her bedroom, putting the long T-shirt back on, but over a bra and trousers now. Al, too, had towelled himself dry and had put his shorts back on, but left off his shirt. His hair he'd rough-dried and it had gone into dishevelled curls. He looked good: masculine and sexy.

They cooked the sardines and ate them with fresh, crusty bread, salad, and tomatoes still warm from the plants that grew in the garden. The wine was cool from the fridge this time, smooth on the palate. Kenzie put on some soft music in the background and Al told her about Hong Kong, the real city, not the commercial centre that it had become. 'You ought to go there,' he remarked. 'Before it gets tidied up out of all recognition.'

'I'd like to. It sounds fascinating.'

'Where do you live? In England, presumably.'

'Yes, in London.'

'And what's this stressful job that you have to get right away from?' He held up a hand. 'No, let me see if I can guess.' They were back on the loungers, although it was almost dark now, and he turned on his side, propping himself on one elbow as he looked at her contemplatively. 'Let me think. I should imagine you work with people; that's why you want peace and quiet.' He raised an eyebrow, but she merely smiled in amusement. 'So you're not going to help me. OK. Then let me think— what kind of people would you most want to get away from? Patients, perhaps. No, I don't think you're a doctor or nurse or you would have told me how to clean up your leg. Children, then.' He looked pleased. 'Yes, that's it. You're a teacher having a blissful holiday away from all the noisy little brats.'

Kenzie smiled. 'Not even close. I'm a—kind of social worker.'

'A *kind* of social worker? Don't they all do the same sort of work, then?'

'Of course not. We all have our speciality.' It wasn't a very good explanation, but Kenzie hoped he'd accept it. She leaned forwards to pick up the bottle of wine, but it was empty. 'Shall we open another?'

'For yourself, of course. But I have to drive back.'

'I won't bother, then.'

Al was still leaning on his elbow, watching her. 'Tell me,' he said, 'were all those things on your kitchen table your own interests?'

'Yes.'

'So you're teaching yourself Portuguese?'

'Trying to, yes.'

'So you must come here a lot to make it worth the bother.'

'Whenever I can.'

'Is it *your* house?'

It was pretty obvious that it must be, so she nodded. 'Yes, I found it when I came here for a holiday a few years ago.'

'Tell me,' he commanded, and settled back on the lounger, his eyes interested as she described the difficulties she'd encountered in trying to buy and renovate the house. Because of her acting background Kenzie was a good story-teller, knowing when to pause for effect, when to raise and lower her voice. Al often chuckled with appreciation, and several times laughed aloud, his laugh rich and masculine. 'But are you the only one who comes here?' he asked when she'd come to an end.

'No, I let friends use it from time to time. That's where the bathing trunks came from,' she felt impelled to say. 'Someone left them behind.'

Al nodded, and as she looked into his face she wondered if he understood why she'd found it necessary to let him know that there was no man in her life.

'Is Al short for Alan?' she asked him.

He smiled a little and shook his head. 'No, I'm afraid it's Alaric.'

'That's almost as unusual as mine. I quite like it.'

'You do?' He raised surprised brows. 'It was the bane of my life when I was at school.'

'I can imagine.' Kenzie smiled and looked away, but she thought, Alaric Rogan. Yes, I do like the name—and I rather like the man.

It was getting late; the daylight had gone completely and they were sitting in the dark, the only light shining through the kitchen window and the still glowing embers of the barbecue. Kenzie began to wonder what would happen next; so far the evening had been on a strictly platonic level and Al didn't seem as if he was going to make any move to change things. OK, he had touched her a few times when they had been playing around in the pool, but there had been nothing at all suggestive in it. Kenzie found she was rather intrigued; in her experience anyone who was attracted to her would have made his feelings quite plain by now.

Under cover of the darkness she was able to give him a contemplative glance. There were few men who had made the grade with her, although a great many had tried. But over the years she had become a master—or should that be a mistress?—of rejection. No, that couldn't be right either; mistresses didn't reject, just the opposite.

Kenzie smiled at the ridiculousness of the thought, and Al said lazily, 'What are you thinking to make you smile?'

She shook her head. 'No reason, really. It's just the wine and the sun and the food.'

'And this house and garden. And being away from care and responsibility.'

'Yes, that too.'

'Contentment then? You must be content to smile for no reason.'

'Yes, perhaps.'

Pushing himself up into a sitting position, his legs between the two loungers, Al reached out and took her hand. Here it comes, Kenzie thought. He's going to suggest we round off a lovely evening by going to bed together. She had worked out three ways of handling a situation like this: the first was to freeze a man out completely with the coldest stare possible, the next to laugh at him in astonishment, saying, 'You!' in complete disbelief. That made them feel *really* small. And the last method was the friendly brush-off, a light remark that left them in no doubt the answer was no, but kept their friendship. This third method was one Kenzie usually used on any man connected with her work who made a pass, people she didn't want to offend by letting them know her true feelings. And then, of course, she could always say yes. But it was too soon, much too soon for that. But there was also maybe, or perhaps.

Kenzie had all these alternatives ready in her mind—she simply had to choose once Al had made his proposition—but he stunned her by pulling her to her feet and saying, 'Come on, we'd better go inside before the mosquitos start biting. I'll help you clear up out here and then we'll do the washing-up.'

Kenzie blinked, not sure whether to be pleased or disappointed. When they'd carried the things inside she said, 'Look, we don't have to do these now, you know. I can do them tomorrow.'

'Why not now? You wash; I'll dry.' And he picked up a tea-towel.

Kenzie turned on the tap, but said drily, 'You're very domesticated.'

'I've been a bachelor for a long time.'

'You're not married, then?'

'No, never have been. How about you?'

She shook her head. 'No, never.'

Al grinned suddenly. 'Well, I'm glad we got that question out of the way.'

The grin was infectious. Kenzie smiled back, any fleeting doubts about his sexuality completely dispelled. 'Didn't you have much opportunity to meet girls in Hong Kong?'

'Girls, yes—but no one I wanted to make my wife.' He dried a glass and held it to the light, watching the rainbow colours given off by the polished facets. 'I imagine you're spoilt for choice in London.'

He didn't look at her as he said it and she didn't know whether it was meant as a compliment or not, so Kenzie decided to be flippant, saying, 'Chance would be a fine thing.'

Setting the glass down, Al turned his head to look at her. He had an attractive voice, with deep tones, and it was warm now as he said, 'Yes, I'm sure a chance with you *would* be a fine thing.'

It was a good compliment, one that wasn't contrived but took advantage of the moment, and was a clever play on words, too. Kenzie appreciated it far more than any fulsome flattery about her looks, or even her brain. The latter seemed to be a popular kind of compliment at the moment; men had been reading about the feminist movement for so many years that they thought nowadays women wanted to be praised for their ability to add figures rather than for their own figure.

Pleased, and a little taken aback by her own pleasure, Kenzie could only smile and say, 'Well—thanks.'

He nodded and went back to his task. 'You're almost out of hickory for the barbecue, by the way.'

'I'll get some next time I go to town.'

'On your bicycle? Don't you have a car?'

Kenzie laughed and shook her head. 'You sound shocked.'

'Don't you feel restricted?'

'Not really. I can always hire a car if I want to go further afield for any reason.'

'How about a radio or television?'

'No, but I have the cassette player for music.'

Al shook his head disbelievingly. 'I know of few modern girls who could shut themselves away like this. You must be one in a million.'

'No,' Kenzie said lightly. 'Just recharging my batteries.'

'That must be some job of yours. You make me feel glad I'm only an ex-whiz-kid, ex-yuppie, work-all-hours common-or-garden banker.'

Kenzie laughed, liking his droll humour and self-deprecation. 'I bet you're very successful,' she guessed.

He didn't enlighten her, just glanced at his watch and said, 'I'd better be on my way. Thanks for dinner.'

'You provided most of it—even cooked it.'

Al's smile almost tempted her to ask him to stay a while longer, but she resisted and led him to the door, and out to his car.

'It was a good evening,' he said as they reached it.

'Yes, I enjoyed it.'

'I'm booked to play golf tomorrow, but would you let me take you out to dinner in the evening?'

Kenzie relaxed a little, only now aware that she had been tensely waiting for him to ask. Which was silly, almost juvenile, but had definitely happened. She smiled. 'Thanks. I'd like that.'

'I'll pick you up at seven, then.' He got in the car, lifted a hand in farewell, and started to drive off—then stopped and came back. 'Kenzie? You never did tell me how much longer you're going to be here.'

She laughed. 'I have over a month longer.'

'Good.' His eyes crinkled into a warm smile. 'I'm glad.' And this time he drove away.

CHAPTER THREE

IT WAS a long time since Kenzie had got so excited over
a date, but somehow this one was special. Maybe it was
because it was her real self, Kenzie Heydon, who had
been asked out, not the worldly and sophisticated television personality Donna Mackenzie. It must be—how
long?—nearly five years since she'd been absolutely sure
that it was for herself that a man wanted to see her again,
not because she was becoming successful. And Kenzie
Heydon, failed actress, was allowed to get excited about
a date with Alaric Rogan, to press a dress and wash her
hair, to make sure her shoes weren't scuffed and to make
up her face. Even to be ready and waiting a good half-
hour too soon, and to feel a ball of nervous tension in
her chest that increased until Al drove up, dead on time.

She became casual then, perhaps a little over-casual,
as she strolled out of the house, merely saying, 'Hi.'

Al gave her a quick, penetrating glance and then his
lips twisted a little in amusement. 'You look great,' he
told her, and she glowed inwardly.

'Thanks.' She didn't tell him that he also looked great,
in cream shirt and trousers, but she certainly thought it.
'How did the golf go?'

'Lost in the morning, won in the afternoon,' he said
cheerfully.

He didn't seem to mind having lost, which was another
plus in Kenzie's estimation. 'Are you a good player?'

'What a question. I have a twelve handicap. Does that
answer your question?'

49

'It doesn't mean a thing,' Kenzie admitted.

He laughed and explained the handicapping system as they drove along. Kenzie had expected him to drive back towards one of the towns on the coast where all the restaurants and nightclubs were situated, but instead Al took a turning inland and drove up into the hills, stopping at a solitary restaurant that overlooked a large lake. It was still light, so they walked down to the water's edge and sat on a seat to watch the sun set over the still water.

'What a lovely place. Is it a natural lake?'

'No, man-made, I'm afraid. There's a dam further along.'

'I've never even heard of the lake, or the restaurant. How did you find it?'

'Somebody who owns one of the other apartments told me about it. We met taking a morning dip the other day.' In a perfectly natural gesture he took hold of her hand in his, entwining their fingers. 'What have you been doing today?'

'Nothing at all exciting.'

'Tell me, anyway.'

Kenzie shrugged. 'I swam and read. Did some painting. Tried to draw a butterfly, but it flew away before I could finish it. Oh, and I walked down to the village to post some letters.'

'Letters?' She felt his grip tighten for a moment.

'Well, postcards mostly. To friends, people I work with,' she said, thinking of her colleagues in Friends in Need. The television people all thought she was in America; and besides, sophisticates like Donna Mackenzie didn't send postcards any more—to them it was trite and old hat.

'How about your family?'

'I don't really have any family. I was an only child. Oh, look!' Kenzie exclaimed as a fish suddenly jumped clean out of the water, its scaly skin turned to brilliant gold in the sunset. It turned in the air, like an acrobat, and dived in again, sending rippling waves that reached out in ever widening circles to the far edges of the lake. She clapped in delight, her face alive with pleasure. 'What an exhibitionist! I didn't know fish could do that. Weren't we lucky to see it?'

She turned excitedly to Al, but grew still as she saw that he was looking at her with a strange, arrested expression in his eyes. But there was more than that; she read surprise, then, even more strange, for a brief instant his whole face seemed to tighten with intense anger. But then it was gone as he smiled, and Kenzie wasn't sure whether she'd imagined it or not. 'I laid it on especially for you,' he told her.

'You have a direct line to the fish in this lake, I suppose?' Kenzie said it lightly, but she was watching him now, wondering if she had been mistaken, or if for an instant she had surprised some deep emotion within him.

But he made a game of it, saying, 'Of course—an underwater fax.'

'Is there such a thing?'

'If there isn't, the Japanese are bound to invent one.' He glanced at the horizon. 'That's the last of the sun, I'm afraid. Let's go and eat. I hope you're hungry.'

'Yes, but somehow I don't think I'll have fish.'

Getting to his feet, Al pulled her up beside him, their hands still entwined. The last golden rays of the sunset lit his face, accentuating the leanness of his cheeks and the firm bone-structure, reminding her of a painting she'd once seen of an Aztec prince. But the prince's eyes had been dark, not this deep, intense blue.

'No, it was much too beautiful, wasn't it?' Lifting his free hand, he placed a long finger against her lips. 'You're very sensitive, aren't you?'

Her heart began to race a little as she opened her mouth to speak, her lips moving against his finger. 'I—I hope so.'

Tracing the outline of her mouth, Al said slowly, 'Is that just to animals—or to people as well?'

'To—to everything, I hope.'

He took his hand away and put it on her shoulder, his eyes holding hers. Kenzie was sure that he was going to kiss her, and she felt a sudden swell of pleasurable excitement, her lips parting a little in anticipation. But then she experienced an equal surge of disappointment as he let her go and turned to start walking up to the restaurant. 'I suppose we all hope that.'

The restaurant was a pleasant place that served good food without making a solemn ceremony out of it, probably because most of the customers were Portuguese and not tourists. They were youngish, too, and wore smart casuals rather than suits. Al and Kenzie avoided the great variety of fish dishes, even though they sounded delicious, and went instead for kebabs, which were brought up on extra-long skewers and hooked onto an old cart-wheel suspended above the table.

'What a great idea.' Kenzie laughed as she pulled some of her food off the skewer and down on to her plate. 'Something as novel as this would go down really well in London.'

'We'll have to pinch the idea and start a restaurant,' Al said lightly. 'We would probably make a fortune—

until everyone else copied the idea and it wasn't a novelty any more.'

Kenzie smiled, but gave him a contemplative look, wondering how important money was to him. 'Are you going back to Hong Kong after your holiday?'

'I'm not sure yet. I might stay in England.'

'In London?'

'Probably.'

'Can you choose?' she asked in surprise.

'To a certain extent. I've done my stint abroad, but I could go somewhere else in the world if I wanted to. Vancouver, probably; that seems to be the up-and-coming place. I'm not confined to Hong Kong or London.'

Kenzie was impressed; he must be good at his job if he was able to pick and choose like that. 'When will you decide?'

He shrugged. 'There's plenty of time yet.' His mouth tightened a little. 'I have some family business to sort out first.'

'Do you have a large family?'

He busied himself with his kebab and didn't look at her as he said, 'Just my mother—and my stepfather.'

'Where do they live?'

'In the South.'

It was a rather terse answer, and Kenzie began to feel as if she were conducting an interview with someone reluctant to talk to her, when the information had to be dragged out of them by incessant questions. 'Will you live with them if you decide to stay in England?'

'Good heavens, no!' That was better; he had opened up on that one.

'But don't you have a home, a base?'

Al paused, thinking about it. 'No, not now. My mother sold up the family home when she remarried, and I got rid of all the stuff I'd left there then. But I was already renting a flat so it didn't make much difference.'

'You got rid of everything from your past, your childhood?'

'Yes, I suppose I did. Does that seem wrong to you?'

Kenzie shook her head. 'I had to do the same after my parents were killed.' She managed to say that quite calmly, really, but went on quickly, 'I lived in digs for a long time after that, so there was no room for any— excess baggage.'

'Where do you live now?'

'I have a tiny flat, not much bigger than a bed-sit, really.'

Al's eyebrows rose. 'But you have the villa.'

'Yes.' Kenzie smiled. 'Most of my spare money goes on that.'

He gave her another of his contemplative looks. 'Forgive me—but haven't you got your priorities wrong? If you only spend a couple of months a year at the villa and all the rest of the time in London——'

'Why don't I spend my money on a better flat?' Kenzie finished for him. 'You've seen for yourself how beautiful the villa is; which would you choose?'

He nodded. 'As you say. But couldn't you let it?'

'No, I don't want to do that,' Kenzie said with a definite shake of her head. 'It's too—precious to me.'

His eyes widened a little at her choice of word. 'But you said that you allow your friends to use it.'

'Yes. From time to time.'

'And you trust them not to abuse the place?'

Kenzie had been lucky in that regard so far. There had been a few breakages, of course, especially when there were children involved, but no one had been so ungrateful or uncaring to do any damage to the house. She shrugged slightly, wanting to change the conversation. 'If you can't trust your friends, who can you trust?'

'That's right, of course.' Al finished his kebab and pushed the plate away. 'How would you like to learn to play golf?'

'I probably wouldn't be any good at it.'

'Why don't you try and find out?'

'I don't have any clubs. And don't you have to have special clothes?'

'You can hire the clubs. And this is Portugal, not Gleneagles; a pair of flat shoes is all you'll need.'

Kenzie tilted her head and gave him a pert look. 'I think I'll need a little more than that.'

He burst into laughter. 'You might at that, otherwise all the other players might be put off their game.' Reaching across, he put his hand over hers. 'Seriously, though, how would you like to try?'

'I think I'd like it very much.'

'Good. We'll start tomorrow.'

Kenzie liked the way he said, 'Good'; it was full of warm approval, as if he'd paid her a compliment, making her feel glad that he was pleased.

They talked of golf and other inconsequential things till the end of the meal, sitting over their coffee and in no hurry to leave. It was only when the restaurant was almost empty that they left and Al drove them back to the villa. The mimosa trees that lined the driveway, their branches heavy with deep yellow flowers, drenched the night with their incredible scent, filling their nostrils as they got out of the car. Moonlight caressed the old walls of the house and silvered the leaves of the climbing roses.

Looking round, Al gave a long sigh. 'Yes, I can see why you love this place so much.'

'The mimosa was one of the main reasons for my buying it.'

He nodded. 'It's incredibly beautiful.' He strolled round the car to stand beside her. 'A fitting frame for you, Kenzie.' She expected him to kiss her then, and he did, but surprised her yet again by picking up her hand and carrying it to his lips. 'Thank you for having dinner with me.'

'No—thank you. I—I enjoyed it.'

'I'll see you into the house.'

He watched her unlock the door and, before she could decide whether or not to invite him in, turned and walked back to the car, but she said, 'Hey, what time tomorrow?'

'Depends how long it takes me to arrange. I'll call you.' He stopped, remembering she hadn't a phone. 'No, I won't. I'll come and collect you.' He lifted a hand in farewell. 'Goodnight, Kenzie.'

'Goodnight. See you tomorrow.'

For the second night running she watched him drive away, but the feeling of regret was far more definite now.

At twenty-seven years old, Kenzie had had more than one love-affair in her life. About four years ago, just before she'd found the villa, she'd even been engaged to be married to a fellow actor, Richard, but he hadn't been able to handle her success. At first it had been OK, although he had tended to treat the whole thing as a joke, and had advised her not to be too disappointed when it all fizzled out. But when she'd begun to deliberately build up the image she'd accidentally stumbled into, and had started to become known and sought-after,

Richard had run her achievements down, sneeringly saying that she was prostituting what talent she had for money. As he was out of work most of the time and the money she was earning had to keep them both, Kenzie hadn't found this very funny. She'd turned on him and said that if she was prostituting her talent, then he was living off the immoral earnings, and if he was too fastidious to do that, then he could go. Her reaction had taken Richard aback, and he had laughed it off. But a couple of months later he'd got a minor part in an Ibsen play at an arts theatre about fifty miles from London, and hadn't invited her to the first-night party, saying that there would only be actors there, implying that she wasn't any longer.

Kenzie could have got angry, but instead she had stayed at home and thought it out. Maybe Richard was right; maybe she wasn't a true actress any more. She had certainly been coming to accept that she would never be a great one. Over the previous couple of years it had become increasingly hard to get acting work, and she'd had to take whatever she could get to earn some money. Luckily she had a very clear and attractive voice, and this had gained her quite a bit of work on local radio; she'd even had a regular slot interviewing local people who'd been in the news. One day Kenzie had waited over eight hours for an acting audition only to be told that the part had been filled even before she'd read for it. She'd even gone to the length of having her hair dyed auburn to try to land the job. Angry, tired and frustrated, she'd arrived at the radio station to do her interview, only to have the interviewee turn up to do the live show at the very last minute, and then to find that she'd been given a man who had recently escaped a criminal sentence because of a legal technicality. He had been rude, sexist and arrogant. After ten minutes of trying to get him to answer her questions, to all of which he'd given a flippant or suggestive answer, thinking himself to be doing the listeners a favour even by being there, Kenzie had flipped her lid. Too angry and fed up to care, she had torn into the man, telling him what she thought of him, his activities and his attitude, finishing with, 'You're nothing but a stupid, ill-mannered lout! Added to which your aftershave makes you stink like a powdered pig!'

Then she had slammed out of the studio, leaving him gaping after her, completely dumbfounded.

Afterwards she could hardly believe what she'd done. In all the earlier interviews Kenzie had conducted she had been kind and interested, taking care to put people at ease and asking them the questions they wanted to answer. She hadn't been able to face the programme producer, but had gone straight home, expecting the phone to ring and to be told that she had been sacked. It had rung, but the producer had been laughing. It seemed they'd had more phone calls from listeners congratulating her than they'd had for any other interview ever before. 'It must have been the red hair,' he'd chuckled. 'Keep it that colour. And keep up that temper,' he'd said. 'I'll find you plenty more where he came from.'

And she had, deliberately developing the angry, sarcastic tone where necessary, and the sugar-sweet innocence that came as the lull before the storm. It was an act, because it was completely opposite to her true nature, but in this at least she was a good actress. Within a year she had started to become known, and she had also taken up writing, often as a crusading journalist. It was then that Richard had got jealous. Pushing emotion aside, which had been far from easy, because she'd thought herself genuinely in love with him, Kenzie had realised that if he couldn't accept what she was doing as her fiancé, then Richard would never accept it as her husband. He was handsome and a good actor, could even be a successful one if he got some lucky breaks, and so long as he had been the one who seemed to be going places everything had been OK between them. Now it wasn't.

Richard, though, hadn't gone so far as telling her to give up the radio work; he had been happy enough to live on the money it brought in while he was 'resting', as being out of work was so euphemistically called in show business. But Kenzie didn't see why the hell she should work to support someone who despised her for doing it, who was even ashamed to be seen with her! The bed-sit they'd been sharing was in her name. Kenzie had packed up all Richard's possessions and got a friend to take them to him. She hadn't even bothered to write and explain; he would probably be pleased to be free of her anyway. Her own things she had moved into the little flat where she still lived. The engagement ring Richard had given her she had donated to Oxfam, figuring they needed it more than either of them.

Since Richard, Kenzie had had plenty of offers from men, but had steered well clear of anyone in show business. She had a theory that success acted like an aphrodisiac, making men want her; or perhaps they just thought that being seen with her would help their own careers. Either way, she was fast becoming cynical about men and sex. Even when she'd been out with men outside the business—always as Donna Mackenzie, of course— there had always been the feeling that they had been showing her off, taking her to places where they would be sure to be seen with her, throwing parties so that she could be introduced to all their friends, that kind of thing. Sometimes Kenzie sardonically felt that she could just send a dummy of herself along and they would be just as happy with that; she certainly hadn't met anyone who she could positively say was interested in her for herself, rather than for what she had become. Until now. Until Al.

Moonlight lay across her bed that night as Kenzie lay awake, thinking about him, but almost afraid to get too excited, too afraid to hope.

He picked her up around ten the next morning and they drove to the golf course near Al's apartment. He had hired a set of clubs for her and took her on to a netted practice area first. 'You should start with the correct grip and everything right from the beginning.'

'What do you mean, "the correct grip"?'

'The way you hold the club. See, like this.' He demonstrated with one of his own clubs, but she didn't get it right, so Al came behind her to put his arms round her and his hands over hers. Kenzie decided there was more to playing golf than she'd ever imagined. He had never been this close before; she could feel the length of his body against hers, his powerful arms enfolding her. Her heart began to thud and she found it almost impossible to concentrate. He moved her hands until he was satisfied she was holding the club correctly, but when Kenzie went to hit the ball she missed completely.

'Relax,' Al advised. 'You're too tense.'

'Really?' She swallowed, tried to forget he was there, and this time managed to knock the ball off the tee.

'No, like this.' Al put his hands over hers and took her through the swing. 'Now you try.'

'Show me again.'

He did so, but then stood back to watch her. Kenzie sighed; it had been good while it lasted. She lined herself up with the ball and this time managed to slice it across the ground.

'That's much better,' Al encouraged. 'Have another try.'

All they did that morning was practise her swing, but by the end of an hour or so she was hitting the balls quite hard into the net.

'That's great,' he told her. 'This afternoon we'll try you on a couple of holes.'

They had lunch in the restaurant at the club. The food was all right, but Kenzie didn't like the place very much; it was too full of tourists, most of them English, any one of whom might possibly have recognised her, despite the fact that she wasn't wearing her auburn wig. And if someone recognised her they would undoubtedly come over to speak and give their opinion of her show. Kenzie had found that out the hard way; with the number of meals that had been interrupted by someone asking for an autograph and talking till her food got cold, she ought to have had chronic indigestion by now.

She was glad when they went outside again. There were two practice holes away from the main course, and Al carried her bag of clubs over. 'Let's walk the holes first,' he suggested.

They strolled along, the grass springy under their feet, the sun hot overhead. When they came to the flag Kenzie looked down at the hole. 'Do you seriously expect me to be able to hit a ball into that ridiculously small hole?'

He laughed. 'That's the general idea.'

'Whoever thought this game up must have been completely mad,' she said firmly. 'Either that or a masochist.'

They came to a large tree and she leaned against the trunk, glad to be out of the sun. Lifting her hand, she took off the sunshade Al had given her and shook her hair loose, immediately feeling cooler. Al, too, leaned against the tree, but his eyes were on her face. 'You're a very attractive woman, Kenzie. And you have a great sense of humour.' He smiled a little. 'I know it wasn't the best way to meet, but I'm glad we did.' Their figures were lost in the deep shade of the tree and it was very quiet, the only sound the endless clicking of the cicadas in the long grass at the side of the course, but this was such a common noise that they didn't notice it any more.

Putting his hands against the tree on either side of her head, he looked deeply into her eyes. Kenzie waited for his own to darken with awareness, with need, but there was a strange, almost detached look in them and in his voice, as he said, 'I think it's about time I did this.' And he bent to kiss her.

It wasn't a passionate kiss. His lips touched hers coolly, moving over her mouth exploringly rather than with urgent desire. It was almost as if he was seeking a response, gauging her reaction, before he committed himself to a full-blown kiss. But to Kenzie it was a foretaste of physical awareness; her heart did a crazy somersault, and a deep ache began to grow within her. She hadn't felt such strong physical desire for a very long time, and it was all she could do to stop herself from putting her arms round his neck, from moving close against him.

When Al lifted his head she slowly opened her eyes and stared up at him. He was watching her, his eyes narrowed. She smiled. 'Do you always do that?'

'Do what?'

'Watch to see a girl's reaction so closely?'

'Was I?' He lifted his finger to trace the outline of her lips. 'With you I think it may be rather important.'

He moved to kiss her again, but they heard voices and saw another couple walking towards them.

'Damn!' Al said with feeling, an expletive that Kenzie echoed in her mind; the day had started to get really interesting.

For the next couple of hours Kenzie developed her swing at the practice holes, and did quite well, considering that her mind kept wandering off what she was doing to the man she was with. She felt extraordinarily happy and full of excited anticipation, like a child who had been promised a great treat. But she was adult enough to know not to be too eager, or at least not to show it. Which was rather difficult when a libido you thought had begun to disappear had suddenly filled your whole body with throbbing awareness. It was just a kiss, she told herself. Hardly even that. And yet it had stimulated desire in her as no other kiss had done for a very long time. But then it wasn't just the kiss; it was Al himself. When she looked at him she felt an inner glow of emotion that she was afraid to define too closely. When he touched her she tingled and wanted more. And she most certainly, definitely, wanted him to kiss her again, just as soon as possible. But she mustn't show these feelings in case he thought her cheap. She must play it cool, as if they had all the time in the world. Kenzie swung at the ball, but sliced it into the rough, so they had to go and look for it.

'I think you've had enough for today,' Al said as he picked it up. 'But you've done really well. Next time we'll try a few holes on the main course.'

She was pleased by his praise, but glad enough to give up. It turned out that Al had hired her clubs for a month, and he put them in the boot of his car with his own. 'We'll take them back to my apartment,' he told her.

Most of the apartment blocks were all too similar, but Al's was one of the better ones. He took her up to the flat with him. It had a largish sitting-room furnished with the modern version of old Portuguese style, not like the rather worn but real thing that Kenzie had at her villa. But there was a balcony that overlooked the swimming-pool and tennis courts, and which was just large enough to take a couple of wicker chairs and a low table.

'Take a seat,' Al offered. 'I'll mix some drinks.'

He didn't ask her what she wanted, but came back with a jug of wine cup. He had changed into shorts, discarding his shirt, and sat in one of the chairs with his feet up on the balcony rail. He looked relaxed, at ease, and she found that she was happy to see him so. Hey, careful, she admonished herself. You hardly know the guy; don't get carried away.

'Have you heard from your friend?' she asked him, to make herself concentrate on something else as much as to make conversation.

'My friend?'

'The one you were supposed to come on holiday with.'

'Oh, no. I didn't expect to.'

'It's a pity he couldn't have let you know he couldn't come earlier. Then you would have been able to invite someone else.'

Al shook his head. 'That's what I thought at the time, but now I'm pleased he didn't.' Reaching over, he took her hand. 'Otherwise I might never have met you.'

'But you would have had a much better game of golf,' Kenzie pointed out with a grin.

Al gave a quick burst of laughter, genuinely amused, and for a moment his grip tightened, but then he let go of her hand as he turned away to refill their glasses. They sat on the balcony for another hour, then Al went to shower and change. While he did so Kenzie used the other bathroom and looked into the spare bedroom. It was completely empty, the twin beds not made up. She could hear Al whistling as he showered, so Kenzie risked a peep into his room, too. This one had a double bed and more wardrobe space, the door hanging open, revealing his clothes. Kenzie was about to turn away when her glance was caught by the professional-looking metal camera and accessory case in the bottom of the wardrobe. There was a small video camera, too. Strange; if Al was so interested in photography you'd have thought he would have produced a camera by now, to take some shots of the villa, at least.

But maybe meeting her had driven photography out of his head, Kenzie thought hopefully. She went back to the balcony, and when he joined her they drove into the town, where they bought some food to cook on the barbecue at the villa. First they swam, but lazily this time, not making a big game of it. If they touched in the water it was accidentally, and Al didn't try to kiss her again. It was as if coming to the villa from the apartment, from the brash outside world to this oasis of peacefulness, had immediately slowed the pace of life again. And also, perhaps, the pace of their relationship.

They ate chicken, done the Portuguese way, and afterwards lay on the loungers, their hands linked, to watch the sunset.

'Does it ever rain here?' Al asked.

'Of course, but mostly in the winter. They have a rule that it never rains when anyone is on holiday.'

Al smiled at the idea, then said, 'In that case we can be sure of another sunny day when we play golf tomorrow.'

Pleased, Kenzie was about to agree, but then remembered that tomorrow was Friday. 'Oh, I'm afraid I can't tomorrow.'

Al's head came round quickly at that. 'Why not?'

Deciding to tease him a little, to see how he would react, as much as anything, she said, 'I have a date.'

'You do?' His face had tightened, and she was rather pleased to see that it was taking an effort for him to appear casual. 'What time is he picking you up?'

'Oh, he isn't; he's coming here. He usually arrives around nine-thirty and stays until four.'

Al's eyes were intent on her face, a slight frown between them now. 'Usually? Is this a regular date, then?'

'Oh, yes. I couldn't possibly break it.'

'And this man; is he English or Portuguese?'

'Portuguese.'

'I see.' His eyes had lost their intensity and were amused now. 'I've an idea I'm being teased. Or is it tested?'

'Now why should I want to do that?' Kenzie said innocently.

'I have absolutely no idea.' But Al lifted her hand to his lips and kissed it, his eyes mocking as he did so. Then he got swiftly to his feet and found a cassette to put on the player. It was dance music, some of it smoochy, some of it fast. Taking her hand, he pulled Kenzie to her feet and into his arms.

There wasn't a great deal of room to dance, but they made the most of it, swinging straight into a trad jazz number. Al was good, taking control, and swinging her round until she was breathless. As an actress, Kenzie had also taken dance lessons, on the basis that the more talents you had, the more opportunities there were for work. She had so enjoyed the physical exercise and also the feeling of well-being that being fit gave her that she had kept up the dancing and aerobics even after she'd given up acting. But by the end of a couple of numbers she was hot and panting, laughing as she clung to Al's arms. She looked up to say something to him, but grew suddenly still as she saw that for the first time there was the darkness of desire in his eyes. The music changed, became slow and intimate. Without speaking, Al drew her close against him, putting both his arms round her as he began to dance again, their bodies as one as they moved to the beat.

Kenzie didn't know how long they danced; sometimes it seemed for a long time, then for just a moment. A great feeling of contentment filled her. It felt right to be held like this in Al's arms, it felt right to be so close, and it also felt right to know that soon they would become lovers. It was completely inevitable, and she was sure that it would be one of the most wonderful moments of her life.

But it wasn't to be that night. When the music stopped Al kissed her, and kissed her properly. His lips were probing this time and soon got the exhilarated response he sought. His arms tightened round her as the kiss deepened, which was just as well as Kenzie was soon lost to all but the dizzying sensations that filled her, making her feel as if the world were whirling round her head and she were falling into some bottomless pool of desire. She put her arms round his neck, clinging to him, and gave a small moan of surprise and sheer delight as her mouth opened under his and she surrendered to the increasing passion of his embrace.

Abruptly he let her go. Kenzie stumbled a little, her arms still around Al's neck, and opened her eyes wide in stupefaction. She had read of kisses that sent you reeling, had even dreamed of them when she was young, but had never, never experienced anything remotely like this reaction in herself before. Lifting her head to stare at Al, she found that he was breathing unevenly, his jaw taut as he strove to control himself. Putting his hands on her arms, he drew them from round his neck, his grip tight. For a moment Kenzie was afraid she'd reacted too strongly, but then he gave a crooked grin and said, 'I think we need a drink. I know I do.'

He poured out a couple of drinks and gave one to her, then sat on the edge of the table and drew her against him, his free arm round her waist. 'The other day,' he said, his voice still unsteady, 'you said that you were here alone "for the moment". Does that mean that someone else is joining you?'

She shook her head. 'No,' Kenzie said softly. 'I said that because—well, because you were a stranger then.'

'But I'm not now?'

'No.' And she bent to lightly kiss his lips, cold from the drink.

'Thank you. And is there anyone—a man—waiting for you back in England?'

Again she shook her head. 'How about you? Did you fall in love with some beautiful Eurasian girl in Hong Kong?'

With sincerity in his voice, Al said, 'There have been women in the past, but it seems that for a long time now I've been waiting for the one girl I want to spend the rest of my life with. Sometimes I thought it was just a dream and I'd never find her. But now...' He smiled and kissed her bare shoulder, then stood up. 'But now

I'm going home. You must get some sleep before this heavy date you've got tomorrow.'

'Al...' She went to reassure him, but he tapped her on the nose with his finger and she knew that it was all right; he was only teasing.

Then he became serious again. 'We have time,' he said. 'And we need to be sure.'

Tonight she was strongly tempted to ask him to stay, but afterwards was glad she hadn't. It had been too intense, that kiss he had given her as they'd danced. In Kenzie it had aroused such deep passions that she would have gone to bed with him there and then. But she saw now that if they had become lovers immediately after it they would have done so with an animal need to satisfy the extreme sexual fires it had inflamed. They would have lost the electric anticipation, the eager, impatient excitement of knowing that they were attracted to each other, of letting their feelings deepen into more than just desire. But there had been so much promise in tonight, in Al's words—and in that kiss. Kenzie strongly suspected that she was about to embark on the most exciting experience of her life. And she also knew in her heart that she was very close to falling in love.

CHAPTER FOUR

KENZIE'S 'date' arrived the next morning, along with his grandparents. The latter were the couple who looked after the house for her when she was away and who came twice a week when she was at the villa to clean the house and work on the garden. Not that either really needed it, but the elderly couple needed the money and their pride would only allow them to work to earn it. Their grandson, Pepé, was seven and wanted to learn English, so, as Kenzie also wanted to learn Portuguese, they taught each other. They took it in turns, twenty minutes' English, twenty minutes' Portuguese, sitting on the terrace while the grandparents worked round them.

They were into their reading session when Al turned up, walking casually round to the terrace. Kenzie wasn't surprised to see him; she had guessed that he would want to check for himself on her date. Her heart began to thud at the sight of him, but she managed to greet him calmly enough. He grinned when Pepé stood up and he saw how small he was, raising his eyebrows as he gave Kenzie a mocking look. He bowed over Maria's hand and was respectful to Antonio. They, in turn, looked him over and must have liked what they saw, because they began fussing around him, Antonio dusting off a seat and Maria bringing him out some of her home-made biscuits that she'd originally brought for Kenzie.

Kenzie looked on with some amusement; Maria was always chiding her for not finding herself a man. Work was abandoned as they all sat and talked until lunchtime.

Al stayed, and praised Maria's cooking so lavishly that she smilingly invited him to the village fiesta the following night.

'Is Kenzie going?' he asked.

'But of course. Senhorita Mackenzie is our guest. As you will be our guest,' Maria said expansively.

It was an unrefusable offer which Al accepted at once. Kenzie would have gone anyway, but it would be perfect now with Al.

After lunch, he got up and came over to put a light hand on her shoulder. 'I came to tell you that I've booked a couple of hours with the pro at the golf course for you for tomorrow morning.'

'I'm that bad, huh?'

Al laughed. 'No! You're that *good*. And will be even better with a pro to start you off right. I would have booked him for you before, but he wasn't available.' His hand tightened on her shoulder for a moment, but he didn't attempt to kiss her with Pepé there. 'I'll call for you at nine-thirty. Bye, now.'

He said goodbye to the others, and as soon as he had gone Maria sent Pepé off on an errand and began to question Kenzie, deeply curious to know more about Al and to find out how close they were.

'He is very beautiful, that one,' Maria said, making a swooning face. 'He would make you a good *marido*.'

'A husband!' Kenzie pretended to be shocked. 'I hardly know him. He was the one who knocked me off my bicycle.'

'Ah! It was *him*?' Maria threw up her hands in amazement. 'Tomorrow I ride a bicycle into town.'

Kenzie laughed, but her face grew serious as she said, 'Do you really like him, Maria?'

Maria had a lot of laughter lines in her face, but she, too, became very earnest as she said, 'Yes, I like him. I think he is good man.' She gave Kenzie a nudge in the ribs. 'I think him will make very good lover.'

Stupidly, Kenzie felt her cheeks begin to flush, and Maria burst out laughing as she went off to the house. Lord, she hadn't blushed in years! Kenzie couldn't even remember the last time. But it felt good. Everything felt good. She felt young and carefree, glad to be alive. All cynicism was gone as she took her first, faltering steps towards the sort of relationship she had begun to think had passed her by forever.

She was ready and waiting when Al collected her the next morning. 'Pepé around?' he asked. When she laughed and shook her head, he put his arms round her and kissed her. 'You taste good.'

'You smell good.'

They grinned at each other like a pair of fools, but then Al said, 'We'd better get going; these pros don't like to be kept waiting,' and drove her to the golf course.

He introduced her to the pro, an Englishman, then said, 'I'll see you in a couple of hours.'

'Aren't you going to watch?'

Al shook his head. 'I might get into trouble for having shown you all wrong.' Then he raised his hand in farewell and went back to the clubhouse.

The pro was pleased with her, but Kenzie would much rather it had been Al again. He worked her hard and by the end of the two hours she was tired and longing for a drink.

'I'm surprised your friend booked you in for a two-hour session,' the pro said as they walked back to the clubhouse. 'I usually only take people for an hour at a time.'

'I think he wants me to get good enough to give him a decent game as soon as possible,' Kenzie answered lightly, but was pleased that Al had done so.

'Well, if you keep on the way you are and get in a lot of practice, you could become quite a good player.'

He said as much to Al, who was sitting on the terrace, waiting for them. Kenzie thanked him and sank into a seat. 'Is that drink for me? Lord, I need it.'

'Worked you hard, did he?'

'And some. You and he are on a par.'

'You're picking up the jargon already,' Al noted with a grin.

She made a face at him. 'What have you been doing?'

'Oh, I've been busy. Reading the papers and chatting, that kind of thing.'

'You poor thing,' Kenzie said with mock-sympathy. 'You must be completely exhausted.'

'I am! I am! Let's go in and have some lunch, shall we?'

'No, thank you.'

He frowned. 'You don't want any lunch?'

'Yes, I would like some lunch, but I would rather not have it here.'

'You don't like this restaurant?'

'Not much. Tell you what; why don't we drive down to the sea? I know a nice *cervejaria* only a few miles away.'

'And just what is a—whatever you said?'

'It's a large café where they serve the most gorgeous seafood snacks and really cold beer.'

Al stood up. 'Just point me in the right direction.'

Their lunch was everything Kenzie had promised, and after it they strolled along the beach until they found a shady spot that wasn't too crowded, then lay down with their heads on Al's shirt and took a siesta.

Later, when Kenzie languidly opened her eyes, she found that Al was sitting up beside her, watching the sea. There was a hard look to his profile, his jaw thrust forwards as if whatever he was thinking about was unpleasant and had to be faced. She remembered him saying that he had some family problem he had to sort out, and wondered if it was that he was thinking about. It occurred to her that she really didn't know a great deal about Al. But then she had known him for such a short time. For a moment that aspect of their relationship disturbed her, but then she remembered that they had spent a lot of time together since they'd met. She could have gone out with a man in London for months and not have been with him so much as she had been with Al. And he had talked openly enough about himself, had seemed to keep nothing back.

A frown creased Kenzie's brows. She was the one who was being secretive. As yet she had made absolutely no mention of her real career, just let Al go on believing that she was a social worker. Once or twice she had toyed with telling him because the opportunity had presented itself, but in her heart she knew that she wouldn't tell him yet. Not until they had become lovers. Not until she was sure that he really cared about her and wouldn't be put off by what she did. He might not be, of course; he might be pleased that she was successful. As yet she didn't know him well enough to be sure how he would react. He ought to be pleased, of course, because what she did was a service to the community, but you could never tell how it might——

'What are you thinking about so pensively?' Al asked, noticing that she was awake.

Taken by surprise, Kenzie said without thinking, 'That I don't know you very well.'

He gave her a long, rather enigmatic look, then picked up her hand and began to play with her fingers. 'No, I suppose neither of us does.'

She sat up, so that their shoulders were touching and she could look into his eyes.

'There are times,' Al said, his tone brooding, 'when people have known each other for a very long time and gradually come to realise that they like each other, and they form a relationship. There are other people who feel an instant attraction and have no need for a long period of getting to know each other first. I rather feel that we fall into the latter category. Don't we?'

The question was important, asking far more than her agreement. 'Yes,' Kenzie said huskily. 'I think we do.'

He nodded, satisfied, but said, 'You must take as much time as you want. I don't want to rush you into anything you're not ready for.' Al laughed suddenly, his face lighting with it. 'Actually that isn't true. And I'm pretty sure you know it.' His eyes holding hers, he said, his voice thickening, 'I want you, Kenzie. I want you very, very badly.'

She gulped a little and nodded, unable to speak, her cheeks colouring beneath her tan. Looking away from him, she picked up some sand and watched as it ran through her fingers. 'But sometimes,' she said with sudden shyness, 'if two people are attracted to each other straight away, when they—they do something about it, then they find that the attraction no longer exists. That it was just—just sex. Do you think it will be like that for us?' She swung her head round to look at him again, surprising a tense, almost cold look in his eyes.

But Al blinked and lowered his head as he kissed her shoulder. 'I hope not,' he murmured against her skin. Then said more clearly as he raised it again and looked into her face, his eyes warm now, 'Oh, Kenzie, my beautiful girl, I certainly hope not.'

They went back to the golf club and played a couple of holes on the large, eighteen-hole course, but then Al dropped her off at the villa and went on to his own apartment so that they could change and go to the fiesta. Kenzie was on a great high of exhilaration, but she managed to remember to go first into the kitchen to fill a watering-can so that she could water her plants, absent-mindedly pushing into place a vase of flowers on the windowsill that wasn't in exactly the place she liked it. That task done, she went upstairs to have a bath and wash her hair, but as she walked into her bedroom she paused, frowning. Something was different. There was an aroma in the air; that was it. She sniffed, but it was fainter now. A musky smell, rather like Al's aftershave. Of course, that must be it. Some of it must have rubbed off on to the clothes she was wearing. Taking off her top, Kenzie held it to her face, but could smell only sand and the sea. She frowned again, then shrugged; the smell had disappeared now so perhaps she had been imagining things.

Ever since she had known that Al was coming to the fiesta, Kenzie had been wondering what to wear. Should she go for something sophisticated or wear the outfit she'd already had in mind? Opening the door of her big wardrobe, her cases piled on top of it, she took out a very full skirt that was mainly black with bands of red. With it she could wear a red silk strapless top and a little black jacket. It was a rather Spanish-looking outfit, but, having been to the fiesta before, Kenzie knew that it would be acceptable. But there was more than the fiesta to think about; Kenzie was certain that tonight Al would take her to bed, and she very much wanted to look good for him, too. For a while she dithered between that outfit and a figure-hugging cream dress, but then decided to wear the black; it was right for the fiesta so she hoped it would be right for Al. Besides, she could wear some of her sexy black underwear beneath it.

She bathed and washed her hair, taking trouble, knowing that tonight would be one of the most important of her life. Like a bride getting ready for her wedding, she thought dreamily as she made up her face, then laughed at herself in the mirror. But oh, lord, she was so happy, so full of expectation. Would Al be a good lover, as Maria had said? she wondered. And then, anxiously, would he be pleased with *her*? But it was a very trivial worry, because somehow she was sure that it would be wonderful. Would fate have gone to all this trouble to bring them together and make them feel this devastating attraction and desire, and not make their lovemaking perfect? Definitely not!

Kenzie laughed again as she twirled in front of the mirror, satisfied that she looked good, and just exotic enough to add extra spice to tonight.

Al arrived on time, and he, too, had dressed for the occasion, in a pale-coloured suit with a darker shirt and a tie. When she opened the door to him he caught his breath, and stood still for a long moment before he slowly let it out again.

Kenzie knew that she had made an impact, but, even so, smiled and said, 'Aren't I what you expected?'

'No!' He said the word forcefully, but then sought to lessen it by smiling and saying, 'You never cease to surprise me. Every time I see you you look more beautiful than before. I didn't know it was possible.'

It was a pretty compliment, but for a moment she didn't take it in, wondering why he had used such a vehement negative. For a brief second doubt came into her mind, but Kenzie quickly shook it off. 'You look pretty fantastic yourself.'

He pretended to be overwhelmed by modesty, making Kenzie laugh. She shut the door behind her and they set out to walk to the village. It was only a small place, but tonight the population had been swelled by friends and relations, and by people from neighbouring villages. Coloured lights hung from all the buildings round the central square and from the palm trees in its centre. Tables had been set out on the pavements and there were three or four lots of musicians playing *fado* music, all seemingly to different tunes.

Pepé had been sent to watch out for them, leading them over to a big table where Maria presided over all her family. Kenzie had met most of them before, but Al had to be introduced and to shake the hand of each one before they sat down opposite each other in the places that Maria had saved for them.

'You must try this port,' Antonio said to Al. 'It is made from the best grapes in the Douro valley.'

'Port before we eat?' Al asked in a low voice to Kenzie.

'They drink it as an aperitif.'

Pepé's sister, who was about fifteen, sat on Kenzie's right side. Leaning towards her, she whispered, 'Your friend, does he speak Portuguese?'

'*Não.*' Kenzie shook her head.

'*Um cavalheiro óptimo,*' the girl observed, giving Al an admiring glance under her lashes.

At the moment Al was talking to Maria, smiling and being an attentive guest. He was completely at ease, had slipped into the circle seated round the table and become a part of it. A couple of the young men there were also good-looking, but to Kenzie's eyes they were nothing on Al. Her heart swelled with pride, and something far deeper that she was humbly grateful to recognise as love. The girl had chosen the right words to describe him; he was, and always would be, her *cavalheiro óptimo*.

There were some other foreigners there, tourists who had heard about the fiesta and wandered into the town, and a privileged few, like Kenzie, who had houses inland and had taken the trouble to get to know their native neighbours and so had been invited along. Earlier in the day there had been a religious procession, but now everyone was relaxed and eager to have fun. But first they had to eat. There were great dishes of meats and seafood, of vegetables and salad. There were lots of Portuguese specialities, too. Al and Kenzie were pressed to eat as if they'd been starving for the whole of their lives. Al asked the ingredients of the Portuguese dishes, but after Kenzie had described dried cod, and squid stuffed with egg yolk, he paled a little and didn't ask any more. There was lots of wine and their glasses were never allowed to empty.

Maria took care that neither Al nor Kenzie felt like strangers. They didn't, but the table seemed awfully wide, the distance between them much too great. The *fado* bands moved into the square and children in national dress danced some of the ancient folk dances, their parents looking on with pride and clapping madly at the end.

Bowls of fruit were brought out and plates of the most delicious pastries, very sweet, but irresistible. Kenzie ate one, then reached out to take some grapes to clear her palate. Al must have had the same idea. Their fingers brushed against each other. Kenzie went to draw back, but suddenly he gripped her hand. Her head came up and she looked into his face. It was the strongest pre-sexual emotion she had ever known. His eyes said it all: desire, need, love. It was almost like the deepest, most passionate kiss, but somehow meant even more than that. The noise of the music and laughter faded, were still there but were of no importance. Looking into his face, Kenzie wanted to tell him that she was falling in love with him, but maybe her own eyes were sending messages, too, because Al's grip tightened convulsively, then he lifted her hand to his lips to kiss it, his eyes still holding hers.

'You have more wine?'

Kenzie turned to answer Antonio and quickly took her hand away. But her heart was thudding, her veins buzzing with inner excitement; she would have felt drunk even without the wine. The adults began to dance now and she and Al were pulled to their feet, joining in the circle of the dance, but not next to each other. Al had long ago taken off his tie and took part with easy enthusiasm as Maria showed him what to do. Kenzie twisted and turned with the other girls, their skirts swirling about them.

For an hour or so things got pretty hectic, the music faster, more than a few people dropping out, some exhausted, some drunk. Then the *fado* players themselves grew tired and they played some slow music. People drifted into couples then, and began to dance together. Al pulled Kenzie to her feet and took her into his arms. He didn't hold her too close, but even so it was close enough for their bodies to touch, to send an electric thrill of anticipation shooting to the core of Kenzie's being. She had never before been so sexually aroused, wanted someone so much. The need to be loved by Al, to be a part of him, was overwhelming. But there was an equal need to give love in return, to give herself and to glory in the giving. For Kenzie was sure now that she loved him, and that he loved her in return. It was what she had always dreamed of: a love that would last and endure for the rest of their lives.

The tension when they touched was becoming too much. But people were beginning to drift away now and it was all right for them to leave, too. They said goodbye to all Maria's family, finishing with her and Antonio, Al complimenting them both on their family, making Antonio look proud and Maria pleased. The older woman looked flushed and tired, and had drunk enough to make her lose her awe of Al. As he shook hands with her she drew him down and whispered something in his ear. He said something in return that pleased her because she smiled and laughed delightedly.

'What did she say to you?' Kenzie asked as Al took her hand and they began to walk back to the villa.

'Our secret,' he responded lightly.

It was nearly a mile to the villa, but the moon was almost full and it was light enough to see. A few cars passed, the passengers honking and waving as some of the revellers went home, but when they'd gone the night became very still, very beautiful. They didn't hurry; Al in fact was going so slowly that Kenzie had to slow her own pace to his. But that was all right; they both knew that they would soon be lovers, and to put it off a little longer only added to the anticipation, would enhance the moment when it came.

Kenzie had thoughts for nothing else, but obviously Al had, because he said, 'I was talking to Maria, asking about her family. Perhaps I misheard her, or didn't understand her properly. I thought she said she had another daughter who couldn't come tonight, that her husband had disgraced her so that she couldn't join in public celebrations.'

'Yes, that's right,' Kenzie answered, somewhat surprised that he'd asked such a question at such a moment. 'Her husband has been in trouble with the police a couple of times.'

'But why should that stop *her* from coming to the fiesta with her family?'

Kenzie gave a small shrug. 'Embarrassment, I suppose. Family shame. Maria and Antonio don't want their neighbours to think they condone what he's done.'

Al let go of her hand and put his in his pocket. 'But that's hardly fair on their daughter. I think it entirely wrong that innocent people should have to suffer because of something their husband or relation has done. Don't you?' The question was hard, direct, in a tone she hadn't heard Al use before.

'Yes, of course. But unfortunately it's a fact of life. Their daughter knew what he was like before she married him. They tried to talk her out of it, but she wouldn't listen.'

'But what if she hadn't known? And what if he goes to prison? Should she be punished because of what he's done?'

'Going to prison is supposed to teach him never to get into trouble again,' Kenzie pointed out reasonably.

'You're dodging the issue.' Coming to a stop, his eyes on her face, Al said, 'If you were a judge, would you send someone to prison if you knew that it would shatter the lives of their family, perhaps make them really ill?'

'If someone has done wrong then he has to be punished for it. You can't let people get away with things because someone else might also have to suffer. The person who committed the crime should have thought of their loved ones before they did it. It's the criminal who has to make the moral decision, not the judge.'

'So you wouldn't show any mercy at all. What if the crime took place a long time ago and had been almost forgotten?'

Kenzie gave him a mystified look. 'What difference does that make? A crime is a crime however long ago it took place.' She gave a short laugh, not liking the way the conversation was going. 'How on earth did we start on such a strange discussion? Can't we talk about something else?'

'Yes, of course. Sorry.' Al's reply was immediate, and he started walking again. 'I felt sorry for Maria, I suppose; she would have liked her daughter to be there.' He put his arm round Kenzie's waist. 'Are we nearly there?'

'A couple of hundred yards.'

'Good.'

They could smell the mimosa before they reached the villa. It was the headiest scent Kenzie knew. When they came to the drive, Al paused to reach up and break a piece off, then held it over her head as if it were mistletoe as he drew her to him and kissed her deeply, deliberately.

Kenzie's legs were still reeling when they got to the front door. Reaching up, she found the key in its hiding-place and put it in the lock.

'You keep a key *there*?' Al's voice was astounded.

'Yes.' Kenzie opened the door. Turning, she put her arms round his neck to kiss him again. 'Would you like to come in?' she said mischievously.

'Just try and stop me.'

Scooping her up in his arms, Al shouldered the door shut and carried her up to her bedroom.

Standing her on her feet, he flicked on the light switch, although the moonlight shone clearly through the window. Coming back to her, Al looked down at her for a long moment, before he put his hand under her chin and tilted her head. Kenzie closed her eyes, expecting another kiss of deepening passion, but he didn't do so at once. Not till she started to open her eyes again did he bend to take her mouth. Kenzie had expected fierce desire and the spontaneity of urgent passion; instead she got a slow, erotic exploration of her mouth, his tongue stroking her lips and probing deeper. It filled her with urgent longing; any kiss at that moment would have done the same. Her pulses raced and she found it difficult to breathe.

'Do you want to use the bathroom?' Al murmured in her ear.

'What? Oh. Yes.' Somehow Kenzie dragged herself back to reality.

In the bathroom she caught a glimpse of herself in the mirror, then stopped to stare at her face. Her eyes were heavy-lidded with desire, her cheeks flushed, mouth parted to let out her unsteady, panting breath. It's the face of someone ripe for love, she thought, and knew that her face hadn't worn that look for a very long time and probably never with such eager intensity.

Al was waiting for her in the bedroom, standing near the bed, and turned towards her as she came in. She paused at the door, waiting for him to stride over, to take her in his arms. But instead he said thickly, 'Come here.'

Slowly she obeyed him. She was trembling with nervous excitement, but even so she could feel the tension in Al's hands as he put them on her shoulders. 'Shouldn't we turn off the light?' she said unsteadily.

'No, I want to look at you.' His hands tightened, but then he released her and stood back. 'Take off your clothes.'

His tone was abrupt. It was a command rather than a lover's plea. It made Kenzie hesitate; this wasn't what she'd expected from him. Looking into Al's face, she saw it pale with tension, the skin drawn tight across his cheekbones and his thrusting jaw. 'Don't you want to do that yourself?' she asked uncertainly.

'No. You do it.' His voice was hoarse now and she saw that his knuckles were white in his clenched fists. Maybe he was shaking too much; maybe he thought that he would spoil things if he fumbled. Her own hands were none too steady either, but she had the advantage of familiarity with the task. The jacket she slipped off her shoulders and dropped on a chair. Al moved away a little and leaned against the wardrobe, his eyes in his taut face devouring her. She wasn't relaxed under his scrutiny, wasn't enjoying this. She turned a little away from him, but Al immediately said, 'No. Let me look at you.'

Reluctantly, feeling shy, she faced him, and began to take off the rest of her clothes. The skirt fell in a dark, glistening heap at her feet, her slip following. She wasn't wearing a bra under the red top. She dropped it on the floor with the others, then stood looking at Al, waiting for him to make a move, expecting him to lunge for her.

But his hands were still balled into tight fists, and his voice was very unsteady as he said, 'Go on.'

She started to shake her head. 'Al, I——'

'*Go on*,' he interrupted fiercely.

'No, I can't.' She was beginning to feel a little frightened now.

But then everything changed. Lifting his hands, Al began to take off his own clothes, unbuttoning his shirt, pulling it off his shoulders, laying bare his broad, tanned chest. Kenzie forgot her own inhibitions then; she took off her panties and ran to help him, pulling at his zip, putting her hands on him and kissing him even before he was free of all his clothes.

He went wild for a while then, kissing her with abandoned passion, bending her against him, letting her know how much he wanted her. She could feel his heart thudding under her hands as she ran them over his chest, hear his harsh, panting breath, feel the sweat of anticipation on his skin. Somehow they were over by the high, old-fashioned bed. Al's hands were on her, exploring, caressing, his panting breath hot against her skin.

She held him off for a moment, looking into his face, wanting to tell him that she loved him. But when she put her hands on his head and tried to turn him to face her, he gave her a quick glance—then looked away.

'Al?'

He put a hand up to his head, wiping sweat from his brow, momentarily covering his eyes. Then he smiled and kissed her again, but more slowly, more deliberately, taking his time. The kiss, so deeply demanding, together with their naked closeness, made her head whirl, her breath catch in her throat. She moaned, and moaned again when he bent to kiss her now sensitive breasts, holding his head between her hands, unable to bear it, but never wanting him to stop. Her moan now was a cry of exquisite delight, of urgent longing for fulfilment.

'I want you,' she cried out. 'Oh, Al, I want you so much!'

Lifting his head, Al opened eyes lost to all but love. Then he gave a long, shuddering groan. Swinging her up, he put her on top of the bed and lay beside her. She kissed him hungrily, her hands deliberately set to arouse him even further, if that was possible. Al let out a cry almost of torment, then, instead of moving on top of her as Kenzie expected, he pulled her on top of him. 'Now!' he commanded hoarsely. 'Now!'

And so it was Kenzie, really, who made love to Al that first time. It was neither what she'd expected from him or wanted. It wasn't the way her dreams had gone. But she was in no position to resist even if she'd been able to. And it gave him such excitement, such groaning pleasure, that she didn't really mind. And almost immediately afterwards Al swung her under him and then it was wonderful for her, too.

Exhausted, they lay in each other's arms, their laboured breathing slowly quieting, the raging heat of their bodies slowly cooling. Kenzie was the first to speak; languidly she said, 'What's that buzzing sound?'

'I can't hear anything.' Al's voice sounded suddenly tense.

'Yes, there's a buzzing noise, like a mosquito.'

'Then perhaps it is a mosquito.'

'They bite,' she pointed out.

Al chuckled. 'So do I.' And he bit at her shoulder, then nibbled her ear lobe.

'Stop it; I can't stand that!' Kenzie exclaimed, loving it.

'So I've found your weakness, have I? What else can't you stand? How about this? Or this?'

Kenzie gasped and moved away from him, caught his hands. 'No, please.'

'Are you going to beg for mercy?' he teased.

Kenzie shook her head. 'No, I trust you. Oh, Al.' She gazed up at him as he leant over her. 'Tonight is the most wonderful of my life,' she said simply.

For a moment his whole face changed, hardened. His brows flickered into a frown and his mouth twisted into something close to repugnance. Kenzie felt a flash of fear, afraid that he didn't want such sentimentality, that she'd said the wrong thing. But then his mouth creased wider and he smiled at her. 'You're as fantastic in bed as you are out of it,' he murmured.

That made her smile. 'We're not actually *in* bed,' she pointed out.

'True.' But he made no attempt to pull back the covers. Instead he sat up and laid her across him with her feet on the floor, facing the wardrobe with its long mirror. Putting his left arm round her, he let his right hand run over her freely, caressing her in the most intimate places, her head lying back against his arm as she sighed and moved voluptuously under his touch. She was soon aroused, soon wanting more than just his hand, and moaned out his name with increasing urgency. But Al twisted round and again took her in a way she didn't expect.

Afterwards, when they again lay side by side on the bed, she said in a voice that was more than half asleep, 'I can still hear that mosquito.'

'I'll catch it.'

She heard Al get out of bed and move around. He clapped his hands together and the noise stopped, then

the light went out. Coming back, he lifted her up a little
to free the covers, then pulled a sheet over her. She expected him to join her, but heard him moving away again.
'Al?'

'In a moment,' he said softly.

Kenzie fell asleep then, physically exhausted, sexually
sated, and didn't stir until the morning sunlight moved
across the bed and touched her face. She woke languidly,
aware that something wonderful had happened. Then
she remembered and was instantly awake, reaching joy-
ously for Al. But the other half of the bed was empty.
Perhaps he was in the bathroom. Quickly she got up,
but saw that the bathroom door was open, and it, too,
was empty. A sick kind of fear filled her, an emotion so
raw that it was close to terror. Kenzie ran downstairs.
The back door was open and she ran out into the garden.
Then stopped, the world righting itself again. Al was
swimming in the pool, as naked as he had been last night.

Almost stunned by relief, Kenzie stood there for a
minute, unable to move. Coming to the end of the pool,
Al turned and saw her. He laughed and stood up, held
out his arms. 'Well, what are you waiting for?'

With a whoop of happiness, Kenzie ran and jumped
into his arms, taking them both under.

Their play in the water was different now. They were
intensely aware of each other's body, were free to touch
wherever and whenever they chose. To rouse and tease,
to kiss and cling.

Hunger drove them out in the end, hunger for love
and hunger for food. They kissed after they came out,
the water coursing from their limbs. Al was so aroused
that Kenzie thought he would want to take her there and
then, but he found a towel and dried her off, then pointed
her towards the kitchen. 'Food first,' he commanded.

She laughed. 'What would you like?'

'Bacon and eggs. I need to recharge my batteries.'

Kenzie didn't need to ask for what. She went into the kitchen, hungry herself. Al came behind her and found her a little apron which he tied round her waist. 'I don't want you getting burnt,' he told her.

He leaned against the door-jamb and watched her, obviously fascinated by the sight of her in the little apron, especially when she bent over to take things from the fridge. When she saw the effect it had on him Kenzie blushed and pushed him out of the door. 'Go and have another swim.'

She carried their breakfast outside, but Al was unable to resist pulling her down on to his lap as she walked by him, so they didn't eat first after all.

The rest of the morning they spent swimming and sunbathing, lying on two lounger mattresses they laid next to each other on the terrace. Kenzie could have stayed there all day, quite expected to, but at twelve Al sat up and said, 'Let's go out to lunch. We'll go to that seafood café we went to before.'

'Don't you want to stay here?' Kenzie asked in surprise.

He put out a familiar hand to caress her waist. 'We have all the time in the world.'

'So we do.' She sat up and put her arms round his neck, looked into his face. 'Darling Al. Thank you.'

'For what?' His voice suddenly sounded rough.

'For last night. For being you.'

She kissed him deeply, lovingly. He made a sound in his throat, then bore her back on to the mattress to make love to her again. And this time it was the most straight-forward and the best, Al seeming to forget his own need as he lifted her to the most exquisite heights of ecstatic excitement, only then allowing himself to take his own pleasure.

Afterwards she cried a little, from gratitude and happiness, and could only say, 'Oh, Al. I didn't know it could be like that. I didn't know.'

He was lying on his back, his hand across his eyes, shielding them from the sun, so she couldn't see his face. 'Go and shower,' he said hoarsely. 'Get dressed. Then we'll go to my place so that I can change.'

Kenzie didn't want to, felt in no state to have to face strangers. She was sure that her new-found happiness would shine out of her like a light and make everyone stare at her. But Al seemed eager to go, and maybe he was right, so she pushed herself up on her feet and went up to her room for a bath. She heard Al come into the bedroom—to dress, presumably—then go quickly down again. A little later she thought she heard his car door slam, but when she looked out of the window he was walking away from it. She dressed quickly, in a casual sleeveless blue blouse and matching skirt, and ran down to meet him.

Al had cleared the patio, locked the door and windows, and was waiting to go.

'All set?'

'Yes—and very hungry.'

'Good.' He smiled down at her as she slipped her hand in his. 'Let's go.'

They drove over to his apartment block, parked the car, and climbed the stairs. The air-conditioning was on, making Kenzie shiver. 'Do you mind if I wait on the balcony?'

'No, of course not.'

He went into his room while she pushed open the windows and went outside. The people from the next-door apartment were out there, too, and the woman immediately got to her feet and came to look over the concrete partition that separated them.

'I thought I heard your doors opening,' she said. 'Have you got the message?'

Kenzie looked at her in bewilderment. 'What message?'

'I don't know what it is; I only know your telephone has been ringing on and off for the past hour.'

'Oh.' A sense of foreboding filled Kenzie's soul. 'I'll—I'll tell him.'

Going back into the apartment, she tapped on Al's door. There was no answer so, guessing he was in the shower, she went into the room and walked across to the bathroom. 'Al.' She banged on the screen.

Turning off the shower, he pushed open the door. 'What is it?'

'I was talking to the woman next door; she says your phone has been . . . ringing all day.' Her words trailed off as the phone began to ring again.

'Can you get it for me? I'll be right out.'

Crossing to the phone beside the bed, Kenzie picked up the receiver. 'Hello?'

'I have a call for you from Hong Kong; hold the line, please.'

Then, after a few seconds, 'Alaric Rogan, please.' It was a man's voice.

'He's just coming.'

She held out the phone as Al came over, a towel wrapped round his waist, his hair rough-dried. 'Hello?' He listened, his face drawing into a frown. 'But surely it can't be that urgent? There must be someone else you can . . . Look, I'm in the middle of my holiday, dammit.' His frown deepened. 'How long for?' Then, 'Are you certain about this? I don't want to leave Portugal unless it's absolutely vital. And I mean that,' he added forcefully.

He talked some more, protesting vehemently, but even before he put the phone down Kenzie knew it would be no good. 'You have to leave,' she said dully.

Al nodded ruefully. 'Yes, dammit. A crisis has come up in Hong Kong. I have to go back there for about a month.' He came to put his arms round her. 'I'm sorry, Kenzie. They really pick their moment, don't they?'

Kenzie didn't ask if it was absolutely necessary for him to go; she had heard him argue and knew that there was no choice. She waited, instead, for him to ask her to go with him, but he went over to the bedside table, looked up a number in a diary, and called the airport, booking a seat for one on the next available plane towards Hong Kong. 'Three-thirty?' He glanced at his watch. 'Yes, I should be able to make that.'

He put down the phone, but Kenzie didn't wait for him to speak. 'I'll help you pack,' she said tonelessly.

'Thanks.' He went back into the bathroom to shave, and finished dressing by putting on a dark business suit. It made him look so different—and yet somehow vaguely familiar.

She took the last things out of his wardrobe and put them in his case, then looked back at the wardrobe and frowned. 'What about your cameras?'

Al had been putting his wallet and things into his pockets, but grew still at her question. 'My what?'

'All the photography stuff you had in the bottom of the wardrobe.'

He straightened up. 'Oh, that. It's already in the car. I meant to take some photos at the fiesta, but I forgot to take the camera.' He smiled. 'I had other things on my mind last night.' Coming over to her, he put his hands on her shoulders. 'I'm incredibly sorry about this, Kenzie. Especially as we were just starting to get really close.'

She gave a short laugh and sighed. 'I was beginning to think it was too good to last.'

He gave her an odd look, but then said, 'It will only be for a month. You should be back in London about the same time as I get there.' He looked at his watch again. 'I'd better get going.'

He drove her back to the villa and got out to say goodbye. 'Sorry about lunch. Sorry about having to leave.'

Kenzie waited for him to say it, but when he didn't she was unable to resist asking, 'Will we see each other again in London?'

Al gave her a suddenly very intense look. 'Oh, yes,' he said forcefully. 'You'll most *definitely* see me again in London.' Taking hold of her shoulders, he gave her one hard, almost fierce kiss on the mouth, then immediately let her go. 'Tell me your phone number.' She did so and he repeated it.

'You'll forget it,' she said anxiously.

He gave her an odd, almost wry look, then said tersely, 'No! I won't forget it.'

Then he was back in the car and driving away, leaving Kenzie standing forlornly looking after him, feeling lonelier than she had ever felt in her life.

CHAPTER FIVE

FOR the first time since she'd owned the villa, Kenzie flew back to England earlier than she need have done. After Al had left nothing seemed the same. Where once she had found peace and tranquillity, she now found loneliness. The hobbies that had filled her hours now bored her after a few minutes. She was restless and couldn't settle to anything. It was, she realised, a classic case of frustration. To have become lovers for just one night, and then to have Al so cruelly taken from her, was enough to make anyone frustrated. She hoped that he would write to her, but no love-letter arrived to delight her heart and reassure her that he still cared. It worried her, and she inevitably began to wonder if Al's feelings went as deep as her own. As the weeks passed Kenzie grew lonelier and her misgivings deeper. When, after four weeks, there was still no word from him, Kenzie couldn't stand it any longer. She packed her bags and got on the first available plane to London.

The flat felt stale, but Kenzie didn't even bother to open a window, rushing straight to the answerphone to see if Al had rung. There were several messages which she listened to impatiently, but Al's deep voice wasn't among them. He hadn't written the number down; maybe he'd forgotten it for all that he'd said he wouldn't. And she didn't know the name of his bank or how to contact him. Kenzie sat down on the floor among her unopened cases and faced the terrible possibility that she might never see him again.

During the next week she grew increasingly despondent. She seldom went out in case the phone rang, rushing to answer it when it did, only to have her hopes sink like lead again when it wasn't Al. She tried to be rational, to tell herself that he was busy, that he'd phone her when he got back from Hong Kong. He'd said a month, but that could easily give or take a few days. Or maybe they'd asked him to stay on for longer. But that didn't stop him from phoning, did it? she immediately thought with angry, frustrated fear. The whole damn colony of Hong Kong must be full of phones. And no one was so busy that they couldn't pick one up and call!

At times Kenzie chided herself for acting like a lovesick schoolgirl with her first boyfriend, but at night in bed alone, and during the day when Al was forever on her mind, she knew that her feelings were those of a woman—a woman who'd found her man and was incomplete without him.

In that case she'd just better set about finding him, Kenzie thought with characteristic determination. Through her office at the television centre, blatantly using her contacts, she made a list of all the merchant banks in London with branches in Hong Kong and Vancouver. As she wasn't sure whether it was a British bank that Al worked for, she also had to list the foreign banks. It was a formidable number, and Kenzie heartily wished that London weren't so popular with the financial world. She toyed with the idea of getting Babs, her secretary, to help her go through the list, but this was too personal; she must do it herself. She tore the list from the fax machine. I'll start tomorrow, she decided, just as soon as the banks open.

Kenzie did so, taking ages to try to get the information she wanted, averaging about half an hour for each bank as she was put through to different departments. 'Call me back when you find out,' she told them, and went on to the next. Again she got nowhere and put the phone down. It rang immediately; the previous bank getting back to her, she surmised, and said shortly, 'Hello.'

'Kenzie?'

She caught her breath as Al's longed for voice spoke her name. She gulped, sick with relief and happiness, and could only stammer, 'Y-yes.'

'It's Al.' Kenzie was too choked up to speak, and he added, his voice quizzical, 'You do remember me, don't you?'

'Yes, of course.' She spoke on a long sigh of thankfulness. 'How are you? Where are you?' And added, because she was so happy, 'God, I've missed you.'

She hoped for, expected, a similar admission from him, but he was silent for a moment before saying, his voice sounding reserved, 'I've been trying to call you, but your line has been busy.'

'Where are you?'

'In London. At the office.'

So *that* was why he couldn't say anything personal; there must be other people around.

'When did you get back?'

'Quite recently.' Which didn't tell her a thing, but then Al said, 'Are you free this evening?'

'Yes, of course,' Kenzie answered immediately, her heart surging with excitement.

'Give me your address and I'll come and collect you.'

She gave it to him, again without hesitation.

'I'll call for you at eight-thirty. See you then.'

'Al?' she said quickly, before he could put the phone down.

'Yes?'

'I—I hoped you'd write to me in Portugal...or phone me here.'

'I had to go to China. It was rather difficult.' He didn't wait for her to make any comment, just said, 'Till tonight,' and rang off.

With a whoop of joy Kenzie tore up the list of banks and ran to her wardrobe to decide what she would wear. And she must wash her hair and tidy the flat, because Al would undoubtedly want to spend the night with her. For once Kenzie wished that she lived somewhere better, but maybe they would go to Al's hotel instead. It didn't matter. Nothing mattered except that they were going to be together again.

By eight she and the flat were as perfect as she could make them. The old Victorian lamp gave out a mellow light over the carved pine bed and its patchwork quilt, brought out the polished gleam of a copper bowl full of bronze chrysanthemums, and the richness of pale green velvet curtains across the deep bay of the window. Wanting to look her best for Al, Kenzie had put on a new designer dress that she had lashed out on just for this moment. It was pale gold in colour, and from the front looked demure enough with long sleeves and a slit neck, but the back was cut into a delicate spider's web of material revealing her bare, tanned back. It had intrigued Kenzie when she had seen it, and she hoped it would have the same effect on Al. Her hair she had put up into a more sophisticated style and fastened with a pearl-encrusted pin that had belonged to her mother.

In the flat above a neighbour began to play a tenor sax. He must have been feeling low; the music he played was sad, melancholy, old blues numbers mostly. Kenzie wanted to shout to him to play something cheerful and triumphant instead. She felt so excited, so happy and eager. The minutes dragged by until her doorbell rang at last. Kenzie ran to open it, her face radiant.

'Al!' She threw her arms round his neck the moment she'd opened the door, hugging him, reaching up to kiss him, not even aware that he didn't put his arms round her, that he wasn't returning her kiss. She let him go at last, laughing, her eyes glistening with tears of happiness. Taking his hand, she pulled him into the flat and shut the door, then immediately went to him again. Smiling up at him, she said huskily, 'It's been so long. I—I've really missed you, darling.'

She put her hands on his shoulders, her fingers on the silky hair where it reached his neck, wanting to touch him, to be close. She was so happy and pleased to see him again that it was only when she looked directly into his face that her smile faltered and she grew still. 'Al?'

'Hello, Kenzie.' There was no gladness in his face. He was looking down at her with a strange, detached look in his eyes. And there seemed to be something different about him; his features were more drawn.

'Is something the matter?'

His brows flickered. 'Family problems.' He held her away from him. 'You look—very sophisticated. Hardly the girl I remember from Portugal.'

'I haven't changed,' she said earnestly, wanting to reassure him. Then, rather painfully, 'Have you?'

Al drew back a little, glanced away, filling her with fear, but then he looked at her again and gave a small crooked smile. 'No,' he said on a definite note. 'I haven't changed, either.'

That should have made Kenzie happy again, but it didn't. She could sense no warmth or spontaneity in him; but then he had been like that in Portugal a few times, throwing up this cool barrier that she hadn't been able to break down. His family problems must be great if they could make him so withdrawn at such a moment. Kenzie was tempted to ask him what they were, but sensed that it would be a wrong move; she must wait until he was ready to tell her himself.

He moved away from her, stood in the middle of the room to look round. 'Is this all of it?' he asked in surprise.

'I also have a small kitchen and a shower room,' Kenzie said defensively.

Al looked at her, seemed as if he was about to ask a question but then changed his mind. 'Do you have a coat or something?'

She nodded and picked up her wrap from the chair near the door. He held the door for her and they went down to the street and over to a car that waited at the kerb. Again Al held the door for her, but he didn't touch her, didn't smile, merely treated her with the common politeness he would have shown to any woman. When they were in the car Kenzie looked at him uncertainly, knowing that somehow everything had gone wrong. This wasn't the way she'd dreamed it, planned it so often in her mind. But she managed to keep her voice light as she said, 'Where are we going?'

His eyes on the road as he drove out into the traffic, Al said in an oddly harsh voice, 'I have a surprise for you.'

'That sounds intriguing. What sort of surprise?'

'You'll see,' he answered, his lips twisting.

There was so much that Kenzie wanted to say, so many things that she wanted, needed, to ask him, but she sensed that he didn't want to talk, and so sat silent, her hands gripped together in her lap under cover of her wrap. Maybe when they got where they were going, when he'd had a couple of drinks and was more relaxed, maybe then Al would tell her what was the matter.

He knew his way round London, driving along one-way streets with a sureness that surprised her when he'd been away for so long. Somewhere in the new Docklands development he drew up in front of an old warehouse that had been converted into flats. 'You've taken a flat here?' Kenzie asked in surprise as they walked to the lift.

Al nodded, punching the button for the sixth floor, the top floor.

'I expected you to be at a hotel. I didn't think you'd have had time to fix up a flat. When *did* you get back to England?' she asked, her eyes searching his face.

But Al didn't answer, instead stepping out of the lift and walking over to the door of one of the flats. Number twenty-seven. Kenzie's heart suddenly began to race. Maybe this was the surprise, the reason why Al was being so mysterious. Perhaps he'd taken the flat for them to share, so that she could move in with him. He unlocked the door and flipped on the lights, and waited while she walked in ahead of him.

It opened into a huge, high-ceilinged room with windows that overlooked the river. The walls were all painted white, acting as a background for several brilliantly coloured modern, abstract prints. The furniture was modern, too, all black leather, glass and straight lines, and there was a communications console with fax, answerphone, computer terminal, the lot. But, dominating the room, there was a television set with the largest screen Kenzie had ever seen in a private home, and beneath it a built-in video system. It was all very glossy, very twenty-first century, but not the kind of place she liked, not the kind of place she would ever want to live in.

Kenzie stood in the middle of the room, taking it all in, then turned to Al, trying to smile. 'Well! It certainly is some surprise.'

'No, the place isn't what I meant. Here, let me take your wrap. Why don't you sit down and I'll get you a drink?' She went to sit over on the sofa, but Al said, 'No, sit here,' and gestured to a chair almost in the centre of the room, in line with the television set.

'Here?' she said in surprise.

'Yes, I have something I want to show you.'

There was a bar with stools in front of it in a raised area at the far end of the room. Going there, Al began to pour a couple of drinks.

'Have you leased this place?' she asked him.

'Yes. Do you like it?'

'No.' She looked across at him, trying to hold his gaze. 'You must know it isn't to my taste.'

To Kenzie's dismay, he shrugged. 'Well, it hardly matters. So long as it serves its purpose.'

'What do you mean?' The chair was low and Al seemed to tower over her as he came to hand her a drink.

'You'll see.' He put his own drink down on a coffee-table by the sofa, then walked over to one of the pictures, moving it aside to reveal a wall safe.

Kenzie stared at his back, wondering what on earth was going on. They should have been at some restaurant by now, holding hands under the table, gazing at each other in the candlelight. And later they would have gone back to his hotel or her flat, to make love all through the night, to tell each other how they'd been missed, and how much they cared.

Al took a small package from the safe, closed it again, and brought it over to her. It was wrapped like a present with a fancy bow. 'This is for you,' he said on an odd note, holding it out to her.

Mystified, but still hoping that the evening was going to come right, Kenzie took it from him. It was about the size of a book, but narrower and lighter. 'What is it?'

'Open it and see.'

Her fingers nervous, Kenzie tore off the wrapping. Inside was a video cassette. It didn't have a label. She looked up at Al questioningly.

Taking it from her, he inserted the cassette in the video machine, then went to sit on the sofa and pick up the remote control. 'Enjoy it,' he said, his voice again oddly strained.

Completely bewildered, Kenzie looked at him for a long moment, then turned her eyes to the screen as the cassette began to play. It was such a large screen that it was almost like being in a cinema, she thought as she watched. First there was a map of Europe, the camera centring on Portugal and then the Algarve. The next shot was of a signpost saying 'Alegre' and a road she recognised. She shot Al a puzzled look, not yet knowing whether to frown or smile. The film ran on, along the familiar road leading to the villa, and there it was, slumbering in the morning sunlight. The camera gave a close-up of the name-plate, 'Villa Mimosa', and went on down the drive.

Was this Al's surprise, then, a pictorial reminder of the villa for her to look at in the dark days of winter?

But then the camera moved inside the house, looked at all the ground-floor rooms and climbed the stairs—into her bedroom. Kenzie was about to ask Al how he'd managed to take the film without her knowing when suddenly it changed from daylight to darkness.

'What happened?' she asked.

'Watch!' It was a terse command.

She turned back to look at the screen just as the light in the villa bedroom suddenly came on and she was there with Al. They were kissing, but then he pushed her away. 'Take your clothes off,' he was ordering.

Kenzie's mouth dropped open as she stared in disbelief, watching as she began to do as he asked, as she went to turn away but he made her face him—and the camera!

Kenzie came to her feet, her face outraged. 'How did you do this? Why have you done it?' Her hopes and happiness crumbling around her, she said in bitter anger, 'What are you—some kind of pervert? A voyeur?'

'What's the matter? You should be used to appearing in front of a television camera. The famous Donna Mackenzie!' Al said it with a snarl, with open contempt in his eyes.

Her face stricken, Kenzie stared at him, her hands balling into fists, her nails digging into her palms. 'You know,' she said in a voice that was slowly becoming aware of deep, raw pain.

'I've always known.' Al's mouth twisted into a sneer. 'Why else do you think I went to all the trouble of getting to know you? And to know you so well,' he added on a malicious note.

Her face devoid of colour beneath her tan, Kenzie turned and strode towards the door, but Al sprang up and caught hold of her.

'Oh, no, you're going to stay and watch till the end.'

'Let go of me!'

Kenzie tried to break free, but he held her easily, enjoying his mastery over her. He let her struggle for a couple of minutes, then propelled her back to the chair and forced her into it. Standing behind her, Al held her shoulders in an iron grip. 'Now watch, damn you!'

Strangely Kenzie wasn't afraid, just full of bitter, heartbroken disappointment at his betrayal. But those feelings were too painful to bear, especially now, when Al was there to see. So she forced them down, made herself feel only anger and contempt, concentrated on them, willed herself to show nothing else. Because to let him see how much he had hurt her would be another pleasure to add to that Al was getting from making her watch. So she sat there stonily and watched as they made love, only now noticing that the cassette film had been doctored so that Al's face was always blurred, only her own showing clearly. A face that was lost in rapture as they made love, moaning softly as he toyed with her as she leaned against the bed, directly facing the camera.

It was at this point that Kenzie deliberately switched her mind off the film. Her eyes might be open, but she was looking inward, forcing her brain to work. The camera must have been concealed on top of her wardrobe, she realised, and that was why Al had made her turn towards it all the time, so that she had been completely exposed to the lens. Humiliation so bitter filled her that Kenzie thought she was going to be physically sick. But she wouldn't give him that satisfaction, and somehow she swallowed it down and forced herself to concentrate again. He must have got into the villa when she wasn't there; she remembered the double-length golf lesson he'd arranged with the pro and realised it must have been then. Other memories came back and she cursed herself for not realising that he'd been there when she'd smelt his aftershave in her room.

She became aware of the screen for a moment and saw that they were making love again. Biting the inside of her lip hard, Kenzie forced herself to show no emotion, to withhold that satisfaction from him. OK, so now she knew how. But why? Well, that was easy enough to answer. There could only be one reason for him to have gone to these lengths. Blackmail.

The screen flickered as the film came to an end. He must have removed the camera when he'd got up in the night. He hadn't filmed them outside when they'd made love straight. Perhaps the tape had run out, she thought with bitter hatred. Or perhaps ordinary lovemaking was just too boring to film.

Above her, Al said harshly, 'Did you enjoy your present?' When she didn't answer, his grip tightened and he shook her. 'Well, did you?'

She didn't look at him, just said shortly, 'What do you want?'

'Oh, but I haven't finished yet. I have another present for you.'

He let her go, but Kenzie didn't make any attempt to run; she knew she would never even make the door. Instead she reached out for her drink with a shaking hand and swallowed it down, badly needing it. Al picked up a photo wallet from a table and held it out to her. Kenzie just looked at him, her eyes full of cold hatred and disgust. Al's glance met hers, and for a moment his brows flickered, but then his chin came up and he emptied the wallet into her lap, the photos cascading down.

'Look at them,' he ordered brusquely.

Slowly she lowered her head, although she made no attempt to pick up the photographs. They had been taken in the garden of the villa the next morning, when they had swum naked and then she had made breakfast with the little apron on—the apron Al had found so sexy that he had pulled her down and made love to her yet again. Another camera hidden in one of the bushes, Kenzie thought dully, and knew then that she would never go back to the villa.

'What do you want?' she repeated. 'How much?'

Al gave a harsh, mirthless laugh. 'Oh, I don't want money.'

Her head came up at that. 'What, then?'

'Do you really think that I went to all the trouble of tracing people who knew you, of finding out that you had a villa near the town, and going to Portugal to try and find you, waiting in the square for days until you turned up, just for money? Is that why you think I deliberately knocked you off your bicycle and made you fall in love with me?'

There was cold anger, venom, in his voice, making Kenzie's heart suddenly fill with dread. It was his coldness that frightened her, not physically, but mentally and emotionally. It chilled her heart, made her terrified of what was to come. Kenzie got to her feet, the photos falling on to the floor, and opened her mouth to deny that she'd fallen in love with him, but then closed it again. She wouldn't degrade herself by lying to him, even about that.

When she didn't speak, he said impatiently, 'Well? Don't you want to know why?'

She gave a thin, painful smile, and said in a voice of contempt, 'I'm sure you can't wait to tell me.'

Al's mouth tightened, but then his jaw thrust forwards as he said, 'Some months ago you did one of your verminous little exposés on a man called Clive Ellison. Ah, yes,' he said with satisfaction when he saw Kenzie's eyes widen. 'I see you remember him.'

'Only because a man wanted to talk to me about him just before I went to Portugal.' She lifted her eyes to meet his. 'I suppose that was you.'

'That's right. But you wouldn't see me. And you wouldn't return my calls to your office.'

'I did, as a matter of fact, but the line was busy.'

Al laughed in open disbelief.

'So what is Clive Ellison to you?'

'My stepfather,' Al said tersely. 'Or what's left of him is—after you crucified him!'

The chill in Kenzie's heart deepened. She couldn't take this; her emotions were too hurt. For the first time in her life she had *known* herself to be deeply in love; what she had felt for her ex-fiancé had been nothing compared to the love she had felt for Al. And she had believed that he cared for her in return, for herself, not her fame and all that went with it. Tonight he had not only betrayed her, but the two sides of her life had been brought crashing into one another, with both of them threatened with destruction. Her own character was too vulnerable, too open not to be broken by it, but Donna Mackenzie, that acerbic, tough and sophisticated woman of the world, could take it in her stride. Turning away from Al, Kenzie closed her eyes tightly for a moment, letting her mind take on the character. It would be difficult without the props—the red wig and the television cameras—but she had been playing the part for so long now that it was like putting on a well-loved coat.

When she turned to face Al again, her chin was up and her green eyes as cold as glacier ice. 'Well, go on,' she said shortly. 'You've obviously been looking forward to saying this for some time, so go ahead, make the most of it—before you sink back into the pool of slime you came from.'

Al's face hardened. 'That attitude isn't going to help you.'

Her lip curved contemptuously. 'I don't *need* help.'

He frowned, not understanding the change in her, then shrugged slightly. 'My mother and stepfather were happy together until your programme ruined their lives. Your cosy exposé! They had both been widowed for many years, both lonely; together they had found real happiness and enjoyment of life again. Until you resurrected the one slip that my stepfather had ever made in his life, a mistake for which he had been trying to atone ever since. For over a dozen years! He thought that it had all been forgotten, that he had been invited on to your programme to talk about the work he does for charity. Instead he had everything raked up in front of millions of people. Do you know what that did to him and my mother? Have you any idea of the anguish you caused?' Al threw the questions at her vehemently, his face dark with anger.

'No,' Kenzie said shortly. She picked up her glass and began to walk towards the bar. 'If this is going to go on much longer I'd like another drink.' It was a remark that would probably only enhance his anger, but she couldn't help it. She had decided that she had to be tough to take this, so tough—and therefore outwardly unfeeling—she was going to be.

Catching her arm, Al spun her round. 'You don't damn well care, do you?'

'I seem to remember we had this conversation once before—in Portugal,' she retorted. 'I wondered why you brought up such an unlikely subject, but obviously you were probing because of your stepfather. What I told you then still stands: if someone has committed a crime they should be punished—no matter how long ago it was.'

'Even though they've tried to make up for it ever since?'

'A crime is a crime,' Kenzie shot back.

'And to hell with the consequences to them or their families!'

'Yes! The consequence is because of their crime, therefore it's their responsibility, not mine.'

His anger overcoming him, Al took hold of her shoulders, gripping hard. 'Do you really see everything as so black and white? Doesn't what a man has done since have any bearing on his case?'

Her face as white and cold as Al's was dark with anger, Kenzie answered curtly, 'Your stepfather thought he had got away with it. It's easy to appear to be good when you haven't been caught or punished.'

'How do you know he wasn't caught? Have you been reading up the case?'

'No. I didn't have to. I would never do a programme on anyone who has already been punished by the law— not unless they were breaking it again. I have no interest in that kind of person.'

'Not sensational enough for you, I suppose,' Al said with a sneer.

'Exactly.' Kenzie threw off his hands and went over to the bar. There was a big mirror behind it but she deliberately didn't look into it, afraid it might put her off the part she was playing. Picking up the nearest bottle, she began to pour some in her glass.

'My stepfather tried to commit suicide.' She froze, whipped by the accusation in Al's voice. 'Overnight, the whole community where he lives turned against him after your character assassination. It didn't matter that for years he'd given of himself unstintingly to help wherever he could, helping the old, raising funds for the hospital, organising charities, serving on the council; in the half-hour it took for your programme to go out, everything he had done was lost. It counted for nothing. Because he'd made one slip nearly fifteen years ago that you'd latched on to.'

He paused and she splashed some tonic into her drink, then turned towards Al again, her features carefully devoid of emotion.

He was standing in the middle of the room, his hands gripping the back of a chair, his fingers digging into the soft leather. 'From being a trusted, respected member of the community Clive Ellison became a—a leper overnight. People he had thought of as friends cut him dead. Organisations for whom he'd worked tirelessly couldn't wait to ask him to resign. All that he'd tried to do to make amends was wasted.'

'What was he working for—an honour from the Queen? A knighthood? Does becoming respectable and doing good works mean that he is to be absolved for past crimes?' Kenzie asked sarcastically.

'I guessed you'd react like this,' Al said on a note close to hatred. 'When I came to watch your last programme and I saw how hard you were, how much you enjoyed destroying lives; I knew then that I had to play just as tough and dirty in return to get what I want.'

So *that* was where she'd seen him before! Oh, God, if only she'd remembered. Biting her lip, she said icily, 'Which is?'

But he shook his head. 'Oh, I haven't finished yet. I want you to know exactly what you did, just what havoc you create in others' lives.' He glared at her, but Kenzie had the strange impression that he wanted to say it for his own sake as much as hers. Did he, then, need to be reassured that what he was doing was justified? 'My stepfather tried to endure the ostracism and he managed to last for several months, but he couldn't take it; his world was in ruins. So he tried to take his own life.' Al paused, and his face became very hard, very bitter. 'But it hadn't only been him who was treated like an outcast. My mother, who is the kindest, best of women, who has never hurt anyone in her life, was treated with equal cruelty. It was she who found Clive after he took an overdose. He recovered, largely because my mother managed to nurse him through it. But the whole thing had made her ill and she had a nervous breakdown. Because of you!'

Kenzie couldn't bear to look at the contemptuous disgust in his eyes. She went to stand by the huge window, looking unseeingly out at the lights of the city spread out before her.

'Well?' Al demanded. 'Have you nothing to say?'

She took a long swallow of her drink before facing him again. 'What do you want me to say?'

'That you're sorry would be a start,' he said on a snarl of renewed anger.

'OK. I'm sorry. Sorry that your mother has become involved and that she's ill. I'm sorry she had the misfortune to marry a man with a past, and who wasn't strong enough to take the consequences. But don't ask me to be sorry for exposing Clive Ellison, because I'm not. Whatever he did, he deserved what he got.'

Al came over to stand near her, to look down at her face. His hands were balled into tight fists, revealing his scarcely controlled anger. 'You can't even remember what it was you accused him of, can you? *Can you*?'

'No,' Kenzie admitted honestly. 'Not the details. He was a builder or something, wasn't he?' She frowned, trying to remember. 'Didn't he put up a building that collapsed and some people were hurt—or even killed?'

'It was an old people's home. An old lady died, but——'

'And you think he should be allowed to get away with it?' Kenzie demanded incredulously.

'*It wasn't his fault!*' Al yelled the words at her. 'He knew nothing about the racket his works manager was operating.'

'He was bound to say that. But everything pointed to——'

'I have proof that he wasn't involved,' Al broke in fiercely, 'proof that it was all done behind his back. His only crime was in trusting his employees too much.'

He said it with utmost certainty, making a *frisson* of fear run down Kenzie's spine; was this the mistake she'd always been in dread of making?

Al must have noticed because he gave a grim smile. 'I tried to contact you with this evidence but you didn't want to know. Well, now I want a complete retraction of your accusations. I want his name exonerated and you to offer Clive a complete apology, on television, on the first programme of your new series. And I want you to tell the viewers just what effect your programme has had on him and my mother. Do you understand?'

She stared at him, then said, 'Yes,' flatly. A look of surprised triumph came into Al's eyes, but quickly disappeared as Kenzie went on, 'I understand what you want, but there's no way I'm going to do it.'

'That's what I'd thought you'd say. Too afraid of losing your reputation with the public—their favourite executioner, selling sex along with the hatchet job. I knew there was no way you would ever admit that you were wrong, let alone that you'd ruined two lives. Two that I know of, that is; heaven knows how many other innocent people you've destroyed during your sordid "vengeance is a right of the viewers" programmes. But this time you're going to *have* to do it.'

'No,' Kenzie repeated firmly.

'You forget the photographs and the tape. If you don't do what I want they'll be sent to the papers. You're a star, a celebrity with a holier-than-thou image; I'm sure the gutter Press will have a field-day destroying your reputation—and with coloured illustrations, too!'

The pain in her heart burned deeper at that, destroying her as no Press attack could, but Kenzie somehow managed to keep her face cold as she said, 'I hadn't forgotten your blackmail. But the answer's still no; I won't say a word about Clive Ellison on my programme until I've seen this evidence for myself and checked its authenticity. Then, if I was wrong, I'll say so.'

Al gave a snort of derision. 'How very high-minded of you. Do you think I can't see through that? The evidence will either get conveniently mislaid, or else you'll keep me hanging on a string indefinitely because you're having difficulty "checking" it. But I'll give you the chance you didn't give my stepfather; you'll have a chance to look at the evidence I have, but it will be held by an impartial solicitor, someone I know I can trust. And you'll have just two weeks to check it out. That should tie in nicely with the start of your new series. And I will write the announcement you'll make then— that's another condition. I don't want you glossing over it as if it's of no importance.'

'You don't want much, do you?' Kenzie said on a sardonic laugh.

'I want justice,' Al retorted, his face hardening. Reaching out, he took her wrist, gripping it. 'I want the just retribution that you say your programme gives to the public. But this time it's the other way round: it's members of the public who want justice from you. My mother and my stepfather.'

'And you're their avenging angel,' Kenzie said with the first trace of bitterness she'd shown for quite some time.

'That's right. And I'm willing to go to any lengths to get it. So, you beautiful little bitch, you'd better do as I want or life will be altogether unpleasant for you. The address of the villa in every paper, no privacy any more, not even in your London flat; I know that address, too, remember? And all the people you've done programmes on—think how they're going to enjoy——'

'All right,' Kenzie broke in shortly. 'You don't have to spell it out. I get the scenario. Now take your disgusting hands off me.'

Anger flicked in his eyes, but then Al gave a grim laugh and let her go. He knew he had the upper hand, that she was in his power. He took a piece of paper from his pocket and gave it to her. 'This is the address of the solicitor who has the documentary evidence. Contact him and he'll give you access to it.'

'And members of my staff.'

Al frowned. 'What do you mean?'

Kenzie gave him a deliberately derisive look. 'You don't think I'm going to bother with something as petty as this myself, do you?'

A murderous gleam came into Al's eyes, but he realised she was goading him and said with silky venom, 'Do take the tape and the photos with you when you go—I've got plenty more copies.'

'No, thanks.' Kenzie strode to the door, paused, and looked back. 'I hope you thought carefully before you decided to start this vendetta... because my job gives me a great deal of power—and I fully intend to use it!'

Al gave a scornful laugh. 'I didn't expect anything else.'

It was becoming harder by the minute to keep up the act. Kenzie knew that she had to get out or she would break down in front of him. And there was nothing now to say, so she merely gave him one last cold look, nodded, and walked away.

CHAPTER SIX

To GO back to the flat and cry her eyes out was a great temptation. It was also completely out of the question. Kenzie called a taxi from the phone booth in the foyer of Al's building and directed it to the television station. Work was the only thing that was going to get her through this crisis, so the sooner she started the better.

There were people on duty at the television centre twenty-four hours a day. Kenzie had to prove her identity to them, but then she was allowed to take the lift up to her office. It was empty at that time of night, although her staff had by now returned from their holidays and were working on the next series of programmes. Kenzie had been into the office a few times since her return from Portugal, but hadn't stayed there for any length of time; she'd been too anxious to get back to the flat in case Al should ring. Pushing that thought determinedly out of her mind, trying not to succumb to the bitterness it brought, Kenzie went to the rack containing video copies of each of her past programmes and ran her finger along the titles. They were filed in date order, which was useful, and she soon found the one marked 'Clive Ellison'.

There were a couple of television and video sets in the main office. Kenzie pushed the cassette into one and settled down to watch. Yes, she'd remembered the interview quite well. Clive Ellison was a man in his late fifties, grey-haired, still good-looking, with a boyish grin of great charm. There had also been an almost saintly earnestness about his manner when he'd spoken of the various charities for which he worked. On the tape Kenzie was listening to him with interest, her attentiveness flattering Ellison and putting him at ease. He had started to become loquacious, gesturing with well-manicured hands, his accent and manner polished, urbane. He had mentioned a large home for disabled children that was being built under his supervision by one of the charities.

It was what Kenzie had wanted. Her face innocent, she had asked him if he'd had much experience of that kind of thing. Cornered, he'd murmured that he'd once been an architect, and had tried to change the subject. But she had been able then to turn on him, reminding him of the old people's home that had collapsed, asking him if he'd told his fellows on the board of the present charity about it. Kenzie had known darn well he hadn't, of course; it had been one of his troubled colleagues who had come to her with the story in the first place.

Ellison hadn't answered directly, had tried to bluff it out, saying she was mistaken, but Kenzie had brought out the cuttings from old newspapers and thrust them under his nose. The circumstances were almost identical; in the previous case, too, he had been entrusted with money from a charity, but substandard materials had been used so that a ceiling had collapsed, killing an old lady who had slept below. When an investigation had been carried out, it had been found that the building had been put up for a quarter of the cost that the charity had paid to Ellison. The balance of the money was never recovered.

'It was not my fault,' Ellison had blusteringly protested. 'No case was ever brought against me. I shall sue for defamation of character.'

'I'm not bringing a case against you now,' Kenzie had pointed out. 'I'm not telling the viewers anything that hasn't already been reported and that they can't read in the papers for themselves. In fact I want to congratulate you on your trustworthiness—your colleagues on the charity must trust you a great deal if they're willing to let you build yet another charitable institution. You have of course told them about the first—incident, *haven't you, Mr Ellison*?'

The man's face had become very white and he had put a hand to his chest. Kenzie recognised the tactic; he would pretend to be ill, having a heart attack or something. Quickly she moved away from him, taking the cameras with her, and closed the interview, finishing with, 'I'm sure that the directors of the charity concerned will give Mr Ellison all the help he needs to ensure that the same—mistake doesn't happen twice. Goodnight, ladies and gentlemen. See you on next week's *Saints or Sinners* show.'

Kenzie rewound the tape, flicked off the television set, then sat gazing at the empty screen. So that man was Al's stepfather. She could well imagine how any woman might fall for him, especially someone who had been alone for a long time. He was good-looking, charming, and seemed eminently respectable. Just like his stepson, Kenzie thought on a sudden wave of bitterness. He, too, had all the looks and charm it took to make her fall for him. She'd been a push-over. Literally a push-over, Kenzie realised cynically as she remembered how he'd knocked her off her bicycle.

She bit her lip, fighting back the tears, and forced her mind to concentrate on Clive Ellison. The file they'd done on him before the interview should still be in the office, in the walk-in safe, presumably. Trying not to

think how Al had opened another safe earlier this
evening, Kenzie tried to remember the current number
to open this one. After a couple of attempts she dredged
up the right combination and found the file. It was a
box file rather than a folder, and was almost full of
papers. They would take a long time to go through, but
Kenzie welcomed that; anything would be better than
having to think of Al.

It crossed her mind to take the file back to the flat,
but that, like the villa, had been ruined for her now. So
she switched on the light in her own office, sent out for
some sandwiches, and settled down to carefully read
through every paper in the file.

It took several hours; there were a couple of taped
interviews to listen to as well as all the written stuff to
go through. When she'd finished Kenzie sat back with
a sigh. If anything, she'd been lenient with Ellison; the
journalist she'd given the job to had gone right back
into Ellison's past, even further than the building fraud.
It wasn't very savoury. In his youth he had left one firm
of architects in the North very suddenly and had had to
move right down to Devon before he'd got another job.
Because it had taken place so long ago the journalist had
only been able to dig up one man, a clerk at the firm,
who'd said that Ellison had been suspected of taking a
small but valuable picture from a house where he'd been
supervising some work. It could have been one of the
workmen, but he was new and they were all old and
trusted employees. Also, only someone with a knowl-
edge of art would have recognised its value, and Ellison
had been in the room where it had been hanging, but
the workmen had not. He had denied it, of course, but
the firm of architects, while keeping the whole thing
hushed up, had immediately got rid of him.

After that he appeared to have kept his nose clean, working for the Devon firm until he had started up his own business, taking a great many of his firm's clients with him, apparently. He had then acted as architect for a great many box-like housing estates and grim tower blocks, cashing in on the building boom. Then had come the old people's home, by which time he was so established that no one had bothered to check what he was doing. Photos taken at the time it had collapsed showed damp ceilings, cracked walls and window-frames that were rotten and twisted. Hardly a place for old people to spend their last days in. But they had bought the small flats within the home because it had had the name of the charity behind it, only to find that all their complaints had gone straight to Ellison, who had merely dumped them in the waste-paper basket.

When the ceiling had fallen in on the old people, it had also fallen on him. He had wriggled like a worm over that, disclaiming any responsibility, blaming everyone but himself, pulling strings, using every contact he had known to get out of trouble—even magnanimously offering to put right the damage out of his own pocket.

The appalled charity organisers, fearful that they would get no more donations from the public, had been willing to accept his excuses and had let him repair the building. Ellison had announced that he was retiring and had sold off his business. The so-called repairs had lasted only two years. When a building inspector had examined the home then he had stated that the only thing to be done with the place was to knock it down and completely rebuild it.

And this was the man Al had gone to such lengths to justify! Kenzie felt a surge of disgust. But she must try to be impartial, to see if there was any chance of her staff having made a mistake. On the face of it there didn't seem much possibility of that. Even given the benefit of the doubt, he had still had the home repaired. If he'd been innocent, as he claimed, Ellison would have made darn sure that those repairs would last, but they had been as shoddily carried out as the original work. It had cost the charity millions in damages and to rehouse the old people who had been left. But the most ironical part of it all was that Ellison's business had been successful enough to give him a comfortable living—it had been sheer greed that had made him act as he had.

Hardly an impartial thought, Kenzie chided herself. Looking at her watch, she saw that it was nearly three in the morning. Apart from the sandwiches, she hadn't eaten, but she didn't feel particularly hungry, or even tired. Mainly she felt a great ache of unhappiness inside, so acute that it was like a physical pain. She supposed that she ought to go home and go to bed, but she knew that she would only lie awake and think of Al, so what was the point? Tomorrow she would get herself some sleeping-pills, but tonight there was only one place to go.

Putting the file back in the safe, Kenzie phoned for a taxi. When the receptionist rang to say it had arrived, she swung her wrap over her shoulders and went down to the foyer. The security people showed no surprise at seeing her alone at that time of night, even in that beautiful dress; they were too blasé to be surprised by anything in their job. The streets were dark and empty as the taxi bowled along, but a light was still on behind the curtains of the upstairs windows of the house where it drew up. She asked the driver to see her safely inside and he obligingly watched as she rang the bell and a tall black man came to open it.

'I thought I'd give you an early night,' she said to the middle-aged woman who guarded Friends in Need's phone.

Her offer was accepted with gratitude and Kenzie took the woman's place, hoping that the phone would soon ring. Others could ring Friends in Need for comfort and a friendly listener, but Kenzie was too hurt to share her own unhappiness and despair, even with the sympathetic friends she had made here. Perhaps especially with them. Some time she would have to think about it, to face it, but not now, not yet. The phone rang and she gave her attention instead to a crying woman whose child had been hit by a car a week ago and had been in a coma ever since. No matter what your own troubles, in Friends in Need you soon found that there were people far worse off.

At eight Kenzie went back to the flat to change into a very businesslike dark suit, and to pack enough clothes for a couple of weeks, then booked into a hotel near the television centre. Back in her office she began to make a great many phone calls. The first few were to several estate agents, asking them to fax through their lists of available properties to the office immediately. Kenzie disliked hotel living and wanted to get a place of her own as soon as possible. Another call went to British Telecom, telling them she no longer required the phone lines at the flat.

That was one place that Al had ruined for her taken care of. The next was going to be far more difficult. The lines to Portugal were nearly always unreliable and it took several attempts before Kenzie managed to get through to the post office in Alegre, and then she had to hold on while someone ran down the road to fetch Maria. The Portuguese woman arrived, breathless and nervous, and it took a while for Kenzie to calm her down and get her to understand that she wasn't coming back to the villa any more. 'I want you to pack up all my clothes and books and give them to charity. I'll send you a list of all the other things I want you to send to me in England when I have an address. I'll let you know what I'm going to do later. No, I'm not sure what I'm going to do with the villa. I'll let you know as soon as I make up my mind. No, of course it's not your fault, Maria. I'm so busy here, that's all. Senhor Al?' Kenzie's hand tightened on the receiver. 'Yes, I've seen him. He—he's fine. No, Maria, I'm *not* going to marry him. Definitely not. Look, I have to go now. Give my regards to Antonio and to Pepé. I'll write to you. Goodbye. *Adeus.*'

Her staff had arrived by now; someone put a mug of coffee on her desk; another brought a file, saw she was on the phone, and dropped it on her desk. Babs brought in the tray of opened letters to be dealt with just as Kenzie put down the phone. 'Are you all right?' she asked. 'You look worn-out.'

'A hectic night,' Kenzie returned with self-mockery.

'Really?' Bab's eyebrows rose; that wasn't an admission that she'd ever heard her boss make before. 'Who were you out with?'

'A man called Clive Ellison.'

'Clive Ellison?' Babs frowned. 'Didn't we do a programme on him?'

'Yes. I spent most of the night reading up his file.'

'Oh, I see.' Babs looked disappointed. 'Why him?'

'Somebody has claimed that they have some fresh evidence about his case.'

'I haven't seen any letter about it.'

'No. The person contacted me personally.' And how, Kenzie thought miserably.

'You often get claims like that. Why don't you let one of the others deal with it in the usual way?'

'I probably will; I had nothing else to do last night.' She picked up the phone again. 'I'll deal with the letters shortly, Babs; I have another couple of calls to make.'

When she was alone again Kenzie called the solicitor whose name Al had given her. He had been warned that she would call, and they arranged for her to come to his office later that morning. Her last call was to a detective agency she sometimes used in the course of her work. 'I want you to do a thorough check on someone for me. I want to know everything about him. His name is Alaric Rogan.' She gave the address of the flat in Docklands, hoping that Al hadn't just borrowed the place for the evening. 'No, I don't have a photograph,' she replied when they asked for one—and that was an irony in itself when Al had been so busy with his own spy cameras. 'I can describe him, though.' She did so and they promised to get someone working on it straight away. 'I want your report brought to me personally,' Kenzie instructed, 'not just handed in at the office.'

That call done, Kenzie sat back in her chair. Her private life and her public life had clashed and she was finding it difficult to know where to draw the line. Al had given her name as Donna Mackenzie to the solicitor, so she supposed she had better go there in that character. Collecting Babs and the letters, she went down to Make-up, and they went through the letters while she had an auburn wig put on and her face done, explaining to the make-up girl that she had to make a personal appearance that day. Which was true enough.

At eleven Kenzie took another taxi to the solicitor's office, going alone. She looked the part she was playing now: tall, slim, glamorous, the auburn hair catching the sunlight, a pair of dark glasses over her lack-lustre eyes only adding to the sophisticated image. A couple of young girls on the look-out for celebrities recognised her as she crossed to the taxi and rushed over to get her autograph. Kenzie gave it with a professional smile, glad that she'd trained as an actress.

When she reached the solicitor's she was shown straight into his office. He rose to meet her—but Al, who was sitting in a chair the other side of the desk, didn't bother. He looked round when she came in, and openly laughed when he saw the wig and glasses.

Kenzie hesitated for a fraction of a second, then shook the solicitor's outstretched hand. Seeing Al so unexpectedly had thrown her badly, but she tried very hard not to let him see it. For a moment his laughter made her feel ridiculous, as if she'd walked on to a stage wearing the wrong costume, but then it made her angry, so it helped. Ignoring Al, she greeted the solicitor with a smile.

'A pleasure to meet you, Miss Mackenzie,' he said with warmth. 'Do sit down.'

'Thank you. I believe you have some documents to show me.'

'Mr Rogan has just brought them along.'

So Al could have shown them to her last night, if he'd wanted. Briefly she wondered why he had come today, but the answer wasn't very hard to find; he wanted to see her reaction when she saw his evidence, wanted to see if she was afraid. What a pity he wasn't going to have that satisfaction, she thought grimly.

Al took a folder from his briefcase and gave it to the lawyer. Inside were two sheets of paper in plastic wallets. The solicitor glanced at them and then passed the first to Kenzie. She took it, aware that Al was watching her closely, and determined to give nothing away. But then he reached across and, before she realised what he was going to do, pulled off her glasses, saying, 'You'll be able to read better without these,' as he did so.

Anger flamed through her. Kenzie almost reached out to try to snatch them back, but in time realised that was probably what he'd hoped she would do. It might even give him an excuse to pull off her wig. Instead of giving him the murderous look he expected, Kenzie managed to smile sweetly. 'Thank you so much.'

Al's gaze searched her face, and she just hoped that the make-up was good enough to cover the dark smudges of disillusion and tiredness around her eyes. It should be; the make-up girls at the television studios were among the best in the world.

Looking down at the document again, Kenzie tried to forget Al as she concentrated on reading it. It was a legal document with the seal of a notary, dated after the interview she'd done with Ellison, she noticed. The sworn statement was by a man, Mark Johnston, saying that he had been employed by Ellison during the building of the old people's home, and that he had been entirely responsible for the work on it. He admitted using substandard goods and taking short cuts to save money. He had kept the balance of the money that Ellison had passed on to him to pay for the work. It finished,

Clive Ellison was completely ignorant of what was going on and is innocent of any charge against him. The responsibility was entirely mine.

Beyond giving a snort of disbelief, Kenzie made no comment, just held her hand out for the other document. This was a signed statement by Ellison saying that he had found out at the time of the accident at the old people's home that Johnston had cheated him and the charity, but, when told that Johnston had taken the money because his wife had needed an urgent operation, he had decided to keep the matter quiet and not prosecute, instead offering his own money to repair the building.

The two documents taken together were disturbing to say the least. Was Clive Ellison so noble that he would take the rap for one of his workmen? Having seen him at his most vulnerable during her interview, having sensed the spite in him behind the urbane façade, Kenzie very much doubted it. It just didn't ring true. Some people might do it to protect a relative or someone close to them, but an employee who had cheated you and ruined your reputation? No way.

Looking up, she said, 'I take it these documents are the originals?'

It was Al who answered. 'Yes, they are—and they're staying in the safe in this office.'

'Am I allowed to have photocopies?'

Again Kenzie addressed the solicitor, who opened his mouth to answer, but again it was Al who said, 'You are—but what good will it do you? You know you've made a mistake, so why not admit it?'

Kenzie gave him a brittle look. 'Why? Have you got a tape recorder hidden in the room to hear me say it? But then, what else could I expect from a piece of slime like you?' she remarked silkily.

The lawyer's mouth dropped open. 'I—er—I'll go and get them copied,' he said faintly.

They were silent until he'd shut the door behind him, then Al rose and came to lean back against the big desk so that he was facing her. He said curtly, 'Throwing dirt at me isn't going to help you.'

'What's the matter—don't you like the truth?'

He gave an angry frown, but then laughed shortly. 'You're like a cornered rat. You know you've lost, but you can't accept it. You're too frightened of losing your reputation with the public.'

'You don't know much about the public, then, do you? Haven't you heard the expression, "No publicity is bad publicity"?'

'I doubt if many so-called saints will be willing to be interviewed by you after those photos are published. And my terms are still the same: I want my account of what happened to be read out and I want a complete apology from you.'

'Why don't you put it in writing?' Kenzie suggested. 'You could get the solicitor to witness it—your family seem to be fond of sworn statements.'

'Because it's their only recourse with uncaring predators like you around,' he retorted swiftly.

Kenzie gave him a contemplative look. 'You seem very convinced of your stepfather's innocence. Have you based your judgement on just these two documents?'

'Aren't they enough?'

'To go to the lengths you did to take those photographs? I'd say no, they weren't.'

'I've spoken to Clive, heard his side. And I've spoken to Mark Johnston, the man who was really to blame for the accident at the home.'

'What did he tell you?'

'Exactly the same as in the document.'

'But he must have gone into far more detail.' She waited for Al to answer, but when he frowned and hesitated she said, 'I want to talk to him myself. I have the right to check on all this.'

The door opened and the solicitor came back in. 'Here we are, Miss Mackenzie, a copy of each one.'

'Thank you.' Kenzie put them carefully into her documents case and took out a notebook. 'I shall need Mr Johnston's address so that I can talk to him.' And she looked at Al expectantly.

He gave her a strange, rather wry look. 'I'm afraid you can't. He died a month ago.'

Kenzie came to her feet. 'You mean that you're relying on the word of a dead man? That it can't be checked or corroborated?'

'That's why he gave the sworn statement,' Al explained shortly. 'He knew he was dying and he wanted to make a clean breast of it.'

'Huh!' She gave a snort of pure derision.

'And just what is "Huh!" supposed to mean?'

'It means that I think your stepfather is lying through his teeth—and you, too, probably. Or else you're so naïve that you can't see when you're being fooled. You want me to go in front of the cameras and apologise because of something cooked up by a cheat and a man who is now, very conveniently, dead! You must be mad!'

'You wouldn't have got any more from him if he'd still been alive. When I saw him to corroborate this, before I went to Portugal, he was extremely ill then and it was enormously difficult for him to talk or write.'

'But you were convinced?'

'Yes—and I don't lie,' Al added acidly.

Kenzie laughed in his face. 'But you sure as hell know how to live one!'

'And what about you?' he shot back. 'I don't remember you ever mentioning your red-haired *alter ego*.'

'Because I wasn't sure I could trust you—and look how right I was proved to be.'

'Ahem.' The solicitor coughed, making them aware of his presence.

Kenzie flushed and dropped her notepad into her case, closing it with a snap. She made to leave, but Al said, 'Don't forget; you have till your first programme.'

'As the man is dead it may take longer than that to check.'

'Tough. The deadline stays.'

'Well, it certainly is a very *dead* line,' she commented drily, and turned away without seeing Al's lips twitch with wry, reluctant amusement at the pun. She nodded to the solicitor, who was holding the door open for her. 'Thank you. Goodbye.'

Outside in the street it was very warm, the sun shining brightly, reflecting from shop windows and the windscreens of passing cars. It made Kenzie remember that Al had taken away her sunglasses. Well, to hell with them; she'd rather buy another pair than ask him for them back. Lifting a hand to shade her eyes, Kenzie looked for a taxi, but couldn't see one. But some passersby saw her, recognised her, and came over to speak. When Al came out of the office building she was signing autographs on scraps of paper, and a curious crowd was starting to gather round her.

'I'm sorry; I have to go now,' she was saying, but a woman caught hold of her sleeve.

'I know someone you can interview. She's a saint if anyone is. Why only the other day she...'

Kenzie saw a free taxi coming and tried to wave to it, but the woman kept hold of her arm. 'I'm sure she sounds wonderful,' Kenzie said placatingly. 'But I really have to go now or I shall be late. Why don't you write to the television centre and tell us all about her in detail?'

'I can't write letters,' the woman said in an aggrieved tone. 'I thought you'd be pleased to hear about her.'

'Of course, but I'm in rather a hurry at the moment.' Looking over the woman's head, Kenzie saw Al lift a hand and catch the cabby's eye. Curse him! The taxi drew into the kerb as she tried to edge away from the woman, not wanting to be rude, but knowing from experience that the woman, excited at meeting a celebrity, would go on and on. Already other people were coming up, wanting to speak, asking for more autographs. Feeling desperate, Kenzie looked round for another taxi, and even contemplated taking a bus.

But then Al pushed through the crowd, firmly removed the woman's hand from her arm, and said, 'So sorry; Miss Mackenzie has to go now. Excuse us.' And he neatly extracted her from the crowd and helped her into the taxi.

Kenzie would have been extremely grateful—if it had been anyone else, and also if Al hadn't got into the taxi after her. The driver pulled away, although she didn't hear Al giving him any instructions.

'Give me my sunglasses,' she demanded.

'Aren't you going to thank me?'

'No. If I'd been wearing my glasses they wouldn't have recognised me.'

'There was another way they wouldn't have recognised you,' Al pointed out.

'You told the solicitor that Donna Mackenzie would be calling; that was who he expected and that was who I had to be.'

'I thought you said you wouldn't be dealing with this yourself?'

'I had an hour to kill. You still haven't given me back my glasses.'

'No.' Al was half turned in his seat, so that he could see her more easily. His eyes were on her face, studying her. 'You look—like another person. Altogether different from the way you were in Portugal.'

'Really?' Talking about Portugal was the last thing Kenzie wanted. Leaning forwards, she told the driver to take her to the television centre.

'That right, guv?' the man asked Al.

'No, go to where I said.'

'Right, guv.'

Her chin coming up in indignation, Kenzie said sarcastically, 'Are you now adding kidnapping to blackmail and coercion?'

'I want to talk to you.'

'But I don't want to talk to you.'

'Unfortunately you don't have any choice.'

'Stop the cab and let me out.' Kenzie reached for the door-handle.

Quickly Al grabbed her arm. 'You little fool; we're in the middle of the traffic.'

'If you don't let me out, I'll scream,' she threatened, really angry now.

Al's eyes narrowed dangerously. 'Just try it.'

Kenzie looked at the width of his powerful shoulders and knew that it wasn't an idle threat. 'I despise men who use their physical strength to intimidate women,' she told him acidly.

'And I despise women who use feminine wiles to get their own way with men.'

'Really? And what are your opinions on men who deceive women for their own ends?'

'What about so-called celebrities who use and intimidate people to further their own careers, regardless
of who they hurt?' Al snapped back.

So they were back at that again. Kenzie realised that
she would never win an argument with Al—let alone intimidate him. He was too strong, too convinced that he
was in the right. His conviction made her uneasy, far
more than the documents he had shown her. If he believed so implicitly in Clive Ellison, then maybe there
was something in his claim after all. She turned away
and was surprised to see the taxi pass the Albert
Memorial and turn into Kensington Gardens.

It drew to a stop and Al opened the door, passing the
driver a note. 'Keep the change.'

'To the television centre now, please,' Kenzie told the
driver, but Al reached inside, took hold of her arm, and
pulled her out after him.

'I told you I want to talk to you. Let's walk.'

'Give me my glasses.'

'So that you can hide behind them?' he asked
sneeringly.

'So that I won't be recognised. I'm a television personality; do you want a crowd to follow us?'

'A *poisonality*, more like.' Al hesitated, but shook his
head. 'That's a chance we'll have to take. I want to see
your eyes, not a pair of oversized glasses.'

Kenzie gave an angry toss of her head and began to
walk along the path between the trees. She felt naked
without the glasses, constantly afraid of giving herself
away. It was too soon to be with him again; she hadn't
yet had time to try to come to terms with his betrayal,
to even let herself think about or feel it very much. The

hurt was there, deep in her heart, just waiting to engulf her. But she mustn't let him see how completely devastated she was; she had to keep up the act, keep on being Donna Mackenzie, and not the pathetic creature that was Kenzie Heydon. It was becoming harder now, though; she was too aware of him, the memories of the one night they had spent together brought to mind whenever she caught the scent of his aftershave, or saw his profile against the sheer blue of the sky. And she was becoming tired, her sleepless night catching up with her.

'What do you want?' she said brusquely.

'You left this behind in my apartment last night.' He took her pearl clip from his pocket and held it out to her.

Kenzie gave a small gasp; she had been so overcome last night that she hadn't even noticed she'd lost it. 'Thank you,' she said on a note of real gratitude. 'It means a lot to me; I would have been very unhappy to lose it.'

'It's of sentimental value?'

'Very much so.'

'Who gave it to you—your fiancé?'

She gave him a quick glance at that. 'Richard? How did you know about him?'

'I looked into your past. It wasn't difficult once I found out that you used to be an actress. I spoke to several people you'd worked with, among them your fiancé.'

'*Ex*-fiancé,' Kenzie emphasised. 'I suppose it was Richard who told you about the villa?'

'What if it was?'

She shrugged scornfully. 'He was always jealous.'

'That wasn't the way he told it.'

'No, I don't suppose it was. Naturally he twisted everything to his own advantage.'

'Naturally?'

Kenzie gave him a contemptuous glance. 'He's a man, isn't he? Or should I say of the masculine gender?'

'There's a difference?'

'Definitely. But you, being the latter, wouldn't know it.'

Al gave her a derisive look, taking that for the insult it was intended to be. He took an envelope from his pocket. 'I wanted to give you this.'

'What is it?'

'The outline of what I want said on your programme when you apologise for maligning my stepfather.'

She didn't take it, instead saying, 'Has it occurred to you that I might be right, that Clive Ellison could have been responsible?'

'In the face of those statements?'

'It's as easy to lie when making a sworn statement as at any other time.'

'A dying man!' Al exclaimed. 'What possible motive could he have?'

Kenzie could think of one, and it was one that she intended to look into, but she merely said, 'We don't just choose people out of the blue, you know; someone has to come to us with the story and then we look into it. Very thoroughly. And we only go ahead with the interview where there is definite evidence against the person. For every "sinner" I interview we probably discard nineteen others. I won't do it unless I'm sure.'

'And you won't admit that you could possibly make a mistake,' he sneered.

'No one is infallible. But I try very hard to be. And I have never been wrong before.'

Al gave her a swift look. 'Are you saying that you might be now?'

'I could be,' she said steadily. 'But so could you. You've shown me your evidence; why don't you look at the file we have on Ellison?'

'I show you mine; you show me yours,' Al quipped sardonically. 'I'm just as adamant as you, Kenzie; I——'

'Don't call me that!' she broke in, on a surge of sudden, vehement anger.

'It's your name, isn't it?'

'My name isn't yours to use—not any more.'

Suddenly it was between them now, the night they had spent together in Portugal, when she had given herself so willingly and cried his name on a great tide of rapture. She had granted this man the freedom of her body, had let him look at her and touch her. His hands had caressed her in the most intimate places, and his lips had murmured her name as they had kissed the softness of her skin. She had been so intoxicated with desire, so wild with passion, that it was difficult to remember the exact words, but she was certain that he had whispered compliments, told her how beautiful he found her. Had she said then that she loved him? Kenzie didn't know, but it was quite probable; she had certainly been sure that she felt it. But Al hadn't said that he loved her, hadn't told her that he cared. All the time he had been using her for his own ends, had felt nothing for her. Except lust. He had felt that all right. No man could have reacted as he had done without being greatly aroused. But even lust hadn't kept him there; he had got what he wanted—and then hadn't been able to wait to get away.

The supreme humiliation of that thought filled Kenzie's heart with bitter hatred. She looked into Al's face and in that moment swore that she would fight this man, bring him down, and make him grovel at her feet!

CHAPTER SEVEN

THERE were no veiling glasses to hide her eyes and Kenzie was unable to control the flood of emotion that filled them. Al gave a small gasp and his face tightened. He made an involuntary movement to catch her arm, but Kenzie swung away from him and began to walk rapidly back towards the street.

'Wait!'

But she broke into a run and waved madly at a cruising taxi. 'Please help me,' she said to the driver as it stopped. 'That man won't leave me alone.'

'Jump in, then, ducks,' he instructed in a strong cockney accent.

Al came up, and put his hand on the door as if to follow her inside, but the driver shot away, making Al jump quickly back out of the way.

'Thanks,' Kenzie said gratefully.

'You're welcome, miss.' He looked at her in his mirror. 'Haven't I seen you before somewhere? Aren't you on the telly?'

Kenzie admitted that she was and he gave her a running commentary on his opinion of her programme, television in general, and of other famous people who'd used his cab. Sitting back in the seat, Kenzie let his voice ride over her. That moment of hatred and determination had been so strong; she must hold on to it, not let it fade. Forget you ever loved him, she told herself; remember only what he's done to you, the way he lied and cheated. And especially remember that once he'd used you he

139

couldn't wait to get away. Al must have arranged for the call from Hong Kong—if it was from Hong Kong—to have been put through to his flat in Portugal when he'd known they would be there and she could answer it. And he'd said he didn't lie! she thought in disgust.

As soon as she reached her office, Kenzie made a phone call, then called in the researcher who had done all the original work on Clive Ellison. He was a young man, only a year out of university, who was hoping to make a career in television.

'Hi, Ben, come in and sit down. I've got a query on the Clive Ellison case. Do you remember it? These documents were given to me by—by a solicitor this morning. He said that we made a mistake and he's demanding a public apology—on television.'

'What?' A worried frown creased Ben's brow. 'But that was such a clear-cut case.' He took the documents and read them. 'But even if these are true, we gave the correct facts as we knew them at the time. And we didn't actually accuse him of anything.'

Kenzie shook her head. 'That's not good enough, I'm afraid. The whole country will think that we've victimised an innocent man. The public are very volatile, Ben; at the moment they love us because we're dragging a lot of dirt from under the carpet, but if they think an innocent person has been wronged then they'll all be on the side of the underdog, and to hell with all the good we've done in the past. So we've got to make absolutely sure that we're right—and we've got to do it fast.'

'You want me to check on it all again?'

'Yes, I do. And I want Tom Williams in on it, too.' Ben looked a little crestfallen, knowing that Tom was their best and most experienced researcher. 'Don't look so glum; we've got to do this as quickly as possible. And two heads are always better than one. Actually, in this case it will be three heads, because I'll be doing a lot of checking myself, but from a different angle. I've already phoned Tom and explained what's happened. As soon as he gets here I want you both to go to the town where these statements were sworn and find out as much as you possibly can about this man Mark Johnston. I want to know if he really is dead, what relatives he left, what money he left, how long he worked for Ellison. Everything you can possibly find, no matter how small. Find out if they were in the same club or lodge. And his wife was supposed to have been ill at about the time that the old people's home was built; it's especially important to find out if that was true.' Kenzie paused, knowing that she'd had no need to spell it all out, that Ben was a very intelligent young man. But this was so important. She had to be absolutely sure of her facts before she faced Al again.

Ben went to leave, but Kenzie said, 'I want you to be fair. If you dig up any facts that corroborate these statements, then I want to know about those, too.'

Ben nodded, unsurprised, and left her office. When he'd gone, Kenzie put her elbows on the desk and her head in her hands, trying to force her mind to think if there was anything more she could do. She would have liked to do all the checking herself, but knew that it would be better to leave it to the more experienced researchers. She was too biased, too eager to find that she'd been right.

The phone rang, her personal phone that didn't go through the switchboard. It was the detective agency. 'We picked up your man this morning.'

'And I suppose you saw him with me,' Kenzie said wryly.

'Yes, we did. So we've got the right man?'

'Yes, you have. He's the one I want to know about. Did you find out if his mother and stepfather are still living at the address I gave you?'

'No, the place is empty. The neighbours said they'd both been ill and had gone away to recuperate.'

'Try and find them for me. It's important.'

'If we can't, nobody can.'

Kenzie wasn't sure about that; Al must have known that she would go all out to check the case, and he would most certainly have removed his mother and her husband to a place where they wouldn't be troubled. She was sure that Al would have done that, sure that he would be protective over his mother. And she could admire him for that, she realised. But then, who the hell wouldn't be protective over their parents? For a moment the old grief engulfed her, and she let it, knowing it was easier that way. It had been around six years now since her parents had been killed together in a freak accident, but sometimes the pain of loss was still almost as sharp and raw as it had been in the beginning. It was shortly after their deaths that Kenzie had got engaged to Richard and allowed him to move in with her. She knew now that she had mistaken her own need for comfort and companionship at that time for love; if the tragic accident hadn't happened she would never have got engaged, never have allowed Richard to get so close to her. But she had been so lonely, so desperately unhappy. Which wasn't much different from the present situation, Kenzie thought with deep bitterness.

She stood up determinedly. This wouldn't do. She needed food and she needed some sleep. If she was going to fight Al, then she needed to be strong. There was a small cloakroom opening off her office. Kenzie used it to change her clothes and take off the red wig, then she borrowed a pair of sunglasses from Babs and went out to eat at a nearby restaurant. She ordered and ate mechanically, giving her body the nourishment it needed, but taking no pleasure or interest in it. The shock of Al's betrayal was beginning to overwhelm her and she knew she couldn't keep it out of her mind much longer. Like Samson without his hair, it was as if she had lost her strength when she'd stopped playing the more dominant role. Pushing her plate away, Kenzie quickly paid her bill and hurried to her hotel, thankfully shutting the door of her room and throwing herself on the bed to give way to unhappiness at last.

When she was weak with crying, sleep came, but it was a troubled, unrestful slumber, and she came awake with a cry after a particularly bad dream. It was seven in the evening, too early to eat again, but too late to go back to the office. Kenzie leaned back against the bed head and thought of the long, empty night that stretched before her. So she had just better fill it. The estate agents she had contacted had faxed through brief details of a great many properties; she had brought them with her from the office and could go through those, set about finding herself somewhere to live.

And there was her future to be thought about and decisions to be made. Decisions, Kenzie realised, that she was reluctant to face because they would involve thinking about Al. Well, if she had to, she had to. The first decision was that the possibility of marriage and a family life was now definitely out. She had trusted only two men in her life and both had let her down; Richard because he couldn't cope with her success, and Al... Kenzie blinked back tears, and angrily told herself she'd done with crying. And done with men. She had been seduced into falling in love and then been betrayed, and there was no way she was ever going to leave herself open to this kind of hurt again. So—men were out! That kind of relationship was no longer a possibility. So she would just have to concentrate on her career.

Her career! Kenzie sighed. If Al gave those photos to the Press she wouldn't have much career left. Briefly she wondered whether he would really do it, then decided that if he was capable of making the threat then he was certainly capable of carrying it out. If she lost her television career, what then? Kenzie knew she would have liked to go to Portugal and shut herself away to lick her wounds, to work on a biography she had started a couple of years ago and had been too busy to finish, perhaps eventually to try to write for television, or a novel, or maybe even a play. Well, OK, the villa was out now; she would never find peace there again, but that didn't stop her from trying to write more, did it? And there were always her celebrity scandal interviews. This was her own idea for a new series of interviews which she had already negotiated to do for radio. They were with well-known people whose lives had been completely changed because of a public scandal. She had taped the series of six interviews before she'd gone on holiday; the powers that be were pleased with them and wanted her to go ahead with another series. The first two interviews had already been broadcast and had received favourable reviews.

This thought giving her some much needed optimism, Kenzie sent down to Room Service for a meal, and decided to divide the rest of the evening between going through the property lists and working out a plan for her future that would cover every eventuality, even that of being shunned by the public. She had taken on a stage-name for her acting career, so what was there to stop her taking a new pen-name for a writing career? Unless Al found it out and betrayed that, too. The unbidden thought, born of unhappiness, came to shatter the small hope for the future and made her cry for a while before she found the strength to try to be positive again.

That night she could only get to sleep by taking a couple of sleeping-pills, a remedy she disliked, but knew that there was no alternative. If she didn't take the pills she would lie awake all through the long hours of the night thinking about Al and just make herself even more miserable. They worked effectively and Kenzie woke feeling much more able to face the day. She had breakfast sent up to her room, and her step was firm as she came out of the lift and strode across the foyer to go to work.

'Good morning.'

The familiar voice made her stop short and her head swing round to see Al getting up from a chair where he had been sitting, reading a newspaper. He folded the paper unhurriedly and came over.

'Nice little bolt-hole you've got here,' he remarked with ironic amusement.

Struggling to control herself, Kenzie said shortly, 'How did you know I was here?'

'Oh, a little bird told me—one of the same species that you hired to follow me. Yours is over in that telephone booth, by the way—pretending to make a call.'

Not bothering to turn and look, or even to deny it, Kenzie said, 'What do you want?'

'I thought I'd walk you to your office, or wherever you're going.'

'Why?'

But Al put a firm hand under her elbow and led her outside before he said, 'You forgot to take the outline of the explanation I want you to give to your viewers.'

'I didn't forget it.'

'But you didn't take it, so it amounts to the same thing.'

Kenzie didn't answer. She tried to shake off his hand, but he wouldn't loosen his grip. 'Let go of me.'

'And have you dive into the nearest cab again? No, I prefer to keep a firm hold on you until I'm ready to let you go.'

'How very macho!' she said contemptuously.

But Al was outwardly very casual this morning and merely smiled a little at the gibe. 'You also forgot these.' He held out her sunglasses. 'Isn't there supposed to be a subconscious reason for a woman always leaving things behind? She wants an excuse to return.'

'And what about a man who refuses to hand things back? What's his excuse—kleptomania?' Kenzie took the glasses and went to put them on, but then changed her mind; she wouldn't let him think that she needed to hide behind them.

'Why have you moved out of your flat?'

'Something put me off going back there—it left a disgusting smell behind.'

Al's face grew grim. 'You're very sparky this morning.'

'Of course. Does that upset you? Did you come to rub salt in the wound?' She managed a mocking laugh. 'What a shame there isn't a wound to rub salt into.'

'You should have kept up your acting career—you're very good. Some people might even have believed that last statement—people who didn't know you rather well, that is.'

'And you think you do?'

'I know you as *intimately* as any man can know a woman.' Al leaned closer as he said it, his voice low in her ear.

The taunt hurt her deeply. She felt like a tortoise that had had its shell ripped off, exposing its vulnerability. Kenzie had never wanted to physically strike someone before, but she would have given anything to hit Al at that moment. Somehow she managed to conquer it, but the look she gave him from fierce green eyes should have shrivelled him. Al merely laughed. It was the laugh that filled her with fury and pushed her into making an indiscreet and untrue retort. 'So what's the big deal? You're not the first one-night stand I've had in my life.'

She had the satisfaction of seeing his face whiten a little and set into grim lines. 'Thanks for telling me; now I really know the kind of woman I have to deal with.'

Kenzie saw the deep disgust in his eyes and turned her head away, biting her lip and cursing herself for having made such a stupid remark. But it was too late to take it back now. Without looking at him, she demanded again, 'Why are you here?'

His voice harsh now, Al said, 'Yesterday you asked me to look at the file you have on Clive Ellison; I've decided to take you up on the offer.'

'Why?'

He shrugged. 'I suppose it's only fair that I should see what you uncovered to make you so sure that he was responsible.'

They had reached the busy main road, lined with cinemas and eating places, that they would have to cross to reach the television centre. The lights were against them and they had to stop and wait as the traffic went noisily by, the air thick with exhaust fumes. Kenzie turned to give Al a contemplative look. 'I'm not sure the offer still stands.'

'Why not?'

'If you read the file it wouldn't make any difference to you. You've convinced yourself of his innocence and are far too narrow-minded and dogmatic to even admit the possibility of your being wrong.'

'That's a very sweeping condemnation—with as much basis of truth in it as your case against Ellison.'

The lights changed and Kenzie strode across the street, her long-legged stride making Al have to step out to keep up with her. When they reached the door of the building, guarded by a uniformed doorman, Al caught her arm. 'Are you going to show me the file?'

She turned to face him, her chin up and a light of battle in her eyes. 'No. It's no longer available. But there's something I will do.'

Al's gaze was on her face, an arrested expression in his own eyes, and it was a long moment before he blinked and said, 'And what's that?'

'Mark Johnston is dead, so we can't talk to him, but there is one other person who knows the truth of what happened when the old people's home was built—Clive Ellison. Why don't we *both* go and talk to him, ask him some questions about what actually happened? Maybe that way we'll discover the truth.'

'He's already given a sworn statement of the truth.'

'A very brief statement. There are a great many more, detailed questions I'd like to put to him.' She paused, but he didn't answer at once. 'Well, what do you say? We could take one of the studio cars now and go together to see him.'

'We couldn't just turn up out of the blue. He's been ill; I'd have to make sure that he would be willing to talk to you.'

'And to you. Have you ever really discussed it with him at any length, gone into detail?'

But Al ducked that one. 'I'll speak to him and ask.'

'OK, but first...' Kenzie opened her bag and took a note from her wallet. 'Here's fifty pounds that says your stepfather will refuse not only to speak to me, but to speak to you as well.' Turning, she gave it to the doorman. 'Harry, here, can hold the stakes. The winnings to go to a children's charity. Does that suit you— or are you afraid to take the bet?' she said mockingly.

Al shrugged. 'If you're so eager to lose your money...' He, too, handed Harry fifty pounds.

Kenzie turned to go in. 'I'll be in my office and I'll be available to go and see Ellison at any time.'

'All right, I'll call you. Will the switchboard put me through?'

'Just ask for extension 2338.'

Kenzie was in her office going through the post for the next couple of hours, but Al didn't call. Then she went to see the producer of her show and told him that when the next series ended she wasn't going to do any more.

'You're afraid that we'll run out of sinners,' he said at once.

'Yes. Most of the sinners we've unmasked have come on because their vanity is so great that they just don't believe it can happen to them. But it will get so that anyone with the slightest secret in their past will refuse to be interviewed, even those we designate as saints. We both knew that the programme could only last for a limited time. When we've done the next six shows, I want to quit.'

'That's fair enough. It's been a good show, Donna, well up in the ratings. Very successful—thanks to you.'

'And to you.' She smiled at him, and for a moment considered telling him about the Clive Ellison investigation, but decided not to unless it was absolutely necessary; it might yet come to nothing.

'Have you any ideas for a new programme?'

'Lots.'

'Good. Let's get together to talk them over some time. How about next week?'

'Fine.'

They arranged to have the discussion over dinner at a good restaurant, and Kenzie wasn't at all surprised when he said, 'Don't forget the wig!'

No, she wouldn't forget it when she went out with him, Kenzie decided, but after the series ended that could go too. The red hair and the temper had carried her this far, but now it was time to find out whether she could carry on without the props. Surely the reputation that she'd built up would be enough even if her hair was dark and her manner not so fiery. Well, it would be an interesting experiment to find out, that was for sure.

She walked back into her office and the first person she saw was Al, perched on the edge of Babs's desk with a mug of coffee in his hands, and chatting away to her secretary as if he had every right to be there. And Babs, showing off her holiday tan in a sleeveless dress, was smiling up at him as if he was God's gift to womankind and had specially singled her out for attention.

He stood up when he saw Kenzie and went to speak, but she said quickly, 'Come into my office,' and immediately closed the door when he'd followed her into the room. 'Who let you in?' she demanded angrily.

'Harry. I told him the bet had been settled.' Al took the hundred pounds from his pocket and held them out to her. 'I'm afraid you win. Ellison refuses to see you.'

'What about you?'

Al's face hardened a little. 'He didn't want to talk to me, either, but he didn't have any choice.'

'You mean—you've been to see him this morning?'

'Yes. I told him he ought to at least give you the chance to talk to him, but he said no. Not after the way you treated him during the television interview. Which is understandable.' He looked at her. 'So I told him that you were checking up on his case because I'd demanded a public apology from you.'

'Hadn't you told him what you were doing?' Kenzie asked in surprise.

'No, I didn't want to build his hopes up prematurely. And besides, I'm not doing it entirely for him; it's largely for my mother.'

'What did he say?' Kenzie asked, watching Al intently. There was something about his manner that made her think that Ellison hadn't been best pleased to hear that Al was taking such an active hand in his affairs.

'He wasn't exactly overjoyed,' Al admitted, leaning against her desk. 'He said that even if you did apologise it wouldn't make much difference, that once dirt like that has been thrown it's almost impossible to wash off completely. Then I told him that I realised that, but that the apology I intend to get from you will completely exonerate him in front of the whole country—and that he can then go ahead and sue you for slander if he wants to.'

'But he said that he wants you to drop the whole thing,' Kenzie said confidently.

Al's eyes flicked to her face. 'What makes you so sure?'

'He's never actually been accused of fraud. It was all hushed up by the directors of the charity. Even in our programme he wasn't directly accused; it was only the insinuations that had been previously published that were used. Now Ellison is afraid that if we do even more checking we might find out that he was *definitely* responsible. He certainly wouldn't want that.'

'You're half right—half wrong. He said that he didn't see any point in my carrying on, that the only proof he had of his innocence was Johnston's sworn statement. He also said that nothing on earth would make you apologise to him even if you did find out that he was speaking the truth—that you would certainly suppress any evidence to that effect if you did find it.'

Kenzie's eyes widened indignantly. 'He obviously judges others by his own standards. What was the outcome?'

'I told him I would carry on to get the apology he deserved. He didn't like it, but he didn't argue when I insisted it was for Mother's sake as well as——'

Al broke off as Babs knocked on the door and then poked her head round. 'Sorry to interrupt. It's your radio producer's secretary on the phone; he wants to confirm that you'll be able to make the party at the Grosvenor this afternoon.'

'Yes, of course.'

'And he wants to know where he should send the car to pick you up and whether you'll be bringing an escort.'

'Tell him my hotel.'

'And the escort?' Babs asked, giving Al a sidelong look.

'No. I'll be alone,' Kenzie said shortly. When Babs had gone she turned to Al. 'Is that all you came to say?'

'Just about.'

'You could have told me all this over the phone.'

'There was the wager.'

'You could have told Harry to pass it on to me.' She gave him a contemplative look. 'I'm beginning to think you can't keep away.'

'You're right,' Al admitted, making her eyes widen. But then he gave her a malicious smile. 'I just can't resist watching you squirm.' He straightened, lifted a hand in nonchalant farewell, and left.

As soon as he'd gone Kenzie rang the detective agency. 'The man you were following; where did he go this morning after he left me at the television centre?'

There was an embarrassed pause. 'I'm afraid we lost him. He gave our man the slip in the traffic. But he was headed north, up the A1.'

'Oh, thanks a lot!' Kenzie exclaimed. 'What am I supposed to infer from that? For all you know he may have doubled back and gone south. But he can't have gone far; he was back at this office within three hours.'

She put the phone down angrily. Trust Al to give his tail the slip. She wondered if he still had someone following her; if so she could hardly go and look for somewhere new to live, not if she didn't want him to know about it. Maybe it would be best if she left that for a while, even though it would mean living in the hotel for longer.

Tom Williams rang in shortly afterwards, but he and Ben had found nothing new. At the end of the morning Kenzie walked briskly back to her hotel, her mind preoccupied. Telling Al that he couldn't keep away had been merely a gibe which he had immediately turned on her, but now she began to wonder if there wasn't something in it. Since he had first contacted her and shown her the video, instead of sitting back and waiting, he seemed to be around all the time. But maybe what he had said was true: he was sadistically enjoying his hold over her.

Feeling dispirited, Kenzie had a snack meal in the hotel, then went up to her room to change for the reception that afternoon. It was to be quite a large affair, a presentation party to mark the retirement of a character in a long-running radio programme. Kenzie had been invited because, long ago, she'd played a role in the series for a few months, and also because there would be quite a few Press people there and her current producer wanted to plug her celebrity scandal series. She went, of course, as Donna Mackenzie, auburn-haired, beautifully made-up, wearing a black suit that had a mannish cut yet somehow managed to look very feminine.

The party was in one of the luxurious function rooms of the Grosvenor. The hired car dropped her off at the entrance, the doorman saluting as he opened the door for her. In the foyer, she paused for a moment to get her bearings, then walked over to the function room, joining a small knot of people who were about to go in.

The retiring actor greeted her at the door with a kiss. 'Donna! Lovely to see you—you're more beautiful than ever.'

She laughed and paid him a compliment in return. 'Why on earth are you taking such early retirement? We all expected you to carry on for another twenty years or so.'

'If only I could. I'll talk to you later.' He turned to greet someone behind her. 'I don't think we've met.'

'No, I'm with—er—Donna. Alaric Rogan. Always admired your work.'

'Thank you. Enjoy yourself.'

Kenzie had swung round and was glaring at Al in infuriated indignation. 'How *dare* you? I'm going to have you thrown out this minute.'

'Nonsense.' Al put a firm arm round her waist and compelled her to move further into the room. 'I'm doing you a favour by acting as your escort—not surprised you couldn't find one, though.'

'Take your hand off me. I only have to yell out that you're a gatecrasher and you'll be thrown out into the gutter where you belong,' she told him, green eyes blazing.

Al flexed his shoulders. 'They could try.' Then he leaned closer so that only Kenzie could hear. 'I have several very interesting photographs in my pocket. How would you feel if I—accidentally, of course—dropped some on the floor? Especially in front of the programme producers?'

'You louse! You stinking——'

'Tut, tut!' Al clicked his tongue. 'Such language from someone who's supposed to be as pure as the driven snow.'

'Donna! There you are.' Her radio producer came over. 'Great to see you. But you haven't got a drink.' He beckoned a waiter over, then looked at Al. 'Haven't we met before? Are you in the business?'

Rightly guessing he meant show business, Al shook his head. 'No. I'm in finance. Alaric Rogan.'

'A broad spectrum,' the producer commented as they shook hands. He frowned, then snapped his fingers. 'Now I remember. You were on a programme I produced a year or so ago, about Hong Kong. You were one of the experts who spoke on the financial aspect of handing Hong Kong back to China.'

'You have a good memory,' Al commented.

'It would have been difficult to forget you—what you said made a great impact.' He glanced at Kenzie. 'Are you here together?'

'No!'

'Yes.'

They both spoke at once.

The producer gave them an amused look, noting Kenzie's flushed cheeks. 'Well, together or not, I'd like to borrow Donna for some Press photographs.'

'By all means,' Al said easily. 'She's very photogenic. I have some good photos of her myself.'

'Where did you meet him?' the producer murmured, drawing her away.

'On holiday,' she answered shortly.

'Well, I'd hang on to him, if I were you. He must be worth a few million.'

'What?' Kenzie stopped to stare at him.

'Didn't you know? His ancestor was one of the partners who started a merchant bank in Hong Kong around the beginning of the nineteenth century. Now it has branches all over the world, and Alaric Rogan is a major shareholder.'

'No, I didn't know,' Kenzie said hollowly.

There was no further time to talk; she had to put on a smile to greet other current and ex-members of the cast, to accept their congratulations—and some ill-hidden envy—at her success. There were publicity photos to be taken, off-the-cuff interviews to give. Several journalists crowded round her, asking about the radio series. Kenzie licked dry lips, wanting another drink. She looked round for a waiter, but it was Al who brought one over and handed it to her. She didn't thank him, just gave him a stony glare. He smiled a little grimly, but stood on the periphery of the group, listening.

'How do you persuade your interviewees to come on the programme?' one journalist was asking.

Still angry, and aware that Al could at any time produce one of his photographs of her in the nude, she answered recklessly, 'I take them out to dinner and give them plenty of wine.' Her chin came up in a challenge as she looked at Al. 'And if that doesn't work I go to bed with them.'

It was taken as a joke and they all laughed, but Al heard and his jaw hardened. He gave her a look of whipping contempt and she waited breathlessly—but he didn't reach into his pocket for the photos. Suddenly Kenzie knew that he had been bluffing, that Al didn't have the photos with him, and that even if he'd had them he wouldn't show them here, because it was too soon, and would deny him the apology he wanted. The threat taken away, Kenzie could relax. Ignoring Al, she finished her interviews and began to circulate. She chatted to several people and then an older woman who had also left the series came over to her. 'A piece of gossip for you, Donna. I ran into Richard, your ex-fiancé, not long ago. He was auditioning for a part in a play one of the touring companies is putting on.'

She paused and Donna gave her the feed-line she wanted. 'What play was it?'

'A trouser-dropping farce! You know the kind of thing.'

'A farce! Richard?'

'Yes, quite a come-down, isn't it? I'd heard he hasn't been doing at all well lately.' The woman grinned, and Kenzie remembered that Richard had once been rude to

her, telling her she was too old for the role she was
playing. 'He didn't get the part, either.'

'I thought he was with the RSC.'

'The Royal Shakespeare Company?' The actress shook
her head. 'Only for a couple of seasons, then he went
into that revival of Ibsen's play, *Ghosts*, but it folded
after only a couple of weeks.' She laughed. 'Maybe he'll
even be trying for a commercial next.'

The woman walked away, leaving Kenzie with mixed
feelings. It wasn't pleasant to learn that someone you
had been close to wasn't doing well, but maybe Richard
had got what he deserved. She joined a group of other
young actors who'd had bit parts in the serial at some
time. A few of them were still in the business; others
had retired for one reason or another—usually because
they couldn't get any work.

They spent some time catching up on each other's
news, then the conversation got round to the sex war.
Al had been talking with a group of men—radio executives, from their age and establishment appearance—
but now the group broke up and he came over to join
the one in which Kenzie stood. There was a momentary
pause as the others all looked him over assessingly, and
Kenzie noticed open interest in more than one female
face. But then one girl, getting back to their conversation, said, 'It's so unfair; men have all the advantages
in the sex war.'

'Only if you let them,' Kenzie remarked. 'Why don't
you make your own rules?'

Before the girl could ask what she meant, Al said,
'What if the man finds out the rules?'

'No man could possibly know all the rules,' Kenzie
said shortly.

'But he could know most of them, and guess the rest.'

She looked at him, realising he wanted a war of words. OK, let him have it, then. Her chin came up. 'If a woman suspects that the man knows the rules she must immediately change some or all of them.'

'That's hardly fair.'

'This is war, *remember*? The rules are subject to change at any time without prior notification.'

Al gave a short laugh. 'A typical female trick. And what if the rules are wrong?'

Kenzie gave him one of her sweetest smiles. 'A woman is *never* wrong.' She added quickly, before he could speak, 'And even if she is, it can only be because of a flagrant misunderstanding which is a direct result of something the man said or did.' Al opened his mouth again, but she swept on, 'For which the man should immediately apologise for causing the misunderstanding.'

The group around them burst into laughter and the women clapped, thinking that she'd won, but Al raised an eyebrow and said, 'What about the man's rules? Or isn't he allowed to have any?'

'Of course he is. But women have known what they are since time began, and they're no more worth the bother of obeying now than they've ever been.'

'Maybe the man had better change *his* rules, then.'

Kenzie shook her head. 'Sorry. The man isn't allowed to change his mind without written consent from the woman—otherwise she might get upset.'

'Aha!' Al made an open-handed gesture. 'Now we've got emotion coming into it. I suppose the woman maintains the right to get angry or upset at any time.'

'You're learning,' Kenzie told him.

'And the man—I take it he has to remain calm at all times?'

Kenzie tilted her head to one side, considering it. 'No, he can get angry and upset, too—but only when the woman wants him to be.'

'And how is the man supposed to know when?'

'Why, that,' Kenzie said on a triumphant note, 'is up to the man to find out.'

They all laughed again, until one girl said, 'But what if they're in love?'

They all looked at Al expectantly, but he in turn looked at Kenzie. 'Well? What's your answer to that one?'

There was a distinct challenge in his tone, and more than a hint of mockery. It made Kenzie remember how he'd seduced her into falling in love with him, just as he'd meant her to. Her voice icy, she said, 'Love? Hate? They're both the same. In those circumstances all rules become null and void.'

'So it's every *man* for himself,' Al said sardonically.

He must have thought he'd won, that he'd had the last word, but Kenzie laughed shortly. 'Isn't that how it's always been? Isn't that why we needed to make these rules in the first place?'

They had come full circle; there was nowhere else for him to go. Al acknowledged it with a small bow, a strange, half-amused, half-angry glint in his blue eyes.

Kenzie immediately moved away and went over to the bar to get a drink, feeling hot and thirsty after their duel of words. She had won, but Al had proved himself a more than worthy opponent, she thought with grudging admiration. At any other time, with anyone else, she would very much have enjoyed such repartee.

As she drank the mineral water, Al came to stand beside her. 'Don't congratulate yourself too much,' he said tauntingly. 'It was only a small battle in a large-scale war.'

'Was it?'

She turned to look him full in the face, her large, expressive eyes fixed on his, her mouth soft and moist, parted a little. For a moment, before Al could hide it, desire showed in his face, darkened his eyes. Then he grew tense, his face mask-like. But it was too late; Kenzie had caught him off guard, and with a feeling of inner exultation knew that he wasn't as immune to her as he made out. Which opened up a whole load of new possibilities.

Setting down the glass, she made her goodbyes and headed for the door. Al followed.

'Where are you going?'

'Back to my hotel.'

'To eat?'

'No, to work.'

'On the Ellison case?' Al asked warily.

Kenzie laughed. 'How obsessed you are! No, I'm going to work on a biography I'm writing.'

'A history?'

'No, a *her*-story.' It was a play on words that made Al grin appreciatively.

They had reached the entrance and the doorman came over. 'A taxi, sir?'

'No, thanks, I have my own car. It's this way.' And, putting a hand under Kenzie's elbow, he walked her down the street. It was chilly now, the sky overcast and grey.

'I'd rather take a taxi.' But she didn't protest too much, at the back of her mind having some idea of testing his immunity, or lack of it, further.

'I dare say, but I want to talk to you.'

'When don't you?' she said with irony.

Al shot her a glance, but they'd reached his car and he held the door for her. It was rather low and her skirt rather tight, but he didn't look away. Getting in beside her, he began to drive, then said, 'Who's the biography on?'

'Aphra Behn.'

She didn't expect Al to have heard the name, but he said, 'The first woman novelist, wasn't she?'

'Yes, she——' Kenzie broke off as the car-phone began to ring.

Al drew into the side and picked up the receiver. 'Hello? Oh, hello, Mother. I'm sorry, I've been away from the car. What's the matt——?' He listened, his mouth growing grim. 'He didn't leave any note or message? Yes, try not to worry. I'm on my way.'

Putting down the phone, Al glanced in the mirror, then did a screeching U-turn in the road, making Kenzie put her hands against the dashboard to steady herself.

'Hey, where are you going?'

'To my mother's place,' Al returned grimly. 'She's in a terrible state; Clive has disappeared and she thinks he may have gone to try to commit suicide again!'

CHAPTER EIGHT

KENZIE stayed silent as Al threaded his way with pur-
poseful skill through traffic building up for the rush-
hour, concentrating on taking advantage of every gap.
When he picked up the M11 motorway, heading north
away from London, he was able to relax a little, and she
said, 'What exactly did your mother say?'

Al's mouth thinned into a grim line. 'It seems that
after I left him this morning Clive told my mother he
was going out for a walk to think things over. He didn't
come back for lunch, but she didn't worry too much,
thought he might have called in at a pub for a meal. But
then they found that a gun was missing.'

'A gun?' Kenzie stared at him in dismay. 'But how
could he have got hold of a gun? Where are they staying,
for heaven's sake?'

'At a friend's house near where Clive used to live. He
keeps several guns for the shooting season.'

Marvellous! Kenzie thought sardonically; they take
someone who's already tried once to commit suicide to
a place where guns are left hanging around. But she kept
the thought to herself, instead asking, 'Didn't they go
and look for him?'

His tone was short, snappy. 'Yes, but it's a large estate
bordering on to Epping Forest—and that covers miles
of ground.'

'Have they called the police?'

'No, not yet. My mother wants me to be there before they do.'

163

'Why didn't you drop me off?'

'Why the hell do you think?' Al snarled at her. 'I want you to see exactly what you've done.'

Kenzie had guessed as much. She sat back in her seat, knowing that there would be no use in pointing out to Al that it was he who had insisted that the case be re-opened. Maybe she had stirred the mud the first time, but now the fault was his. And she had great reservations about the whole thing. Although willing to allow that his mother's distress would be genuine, she very much doubted if Clive Ellison was the type to take his own life; she was sure that he wanted this new investigation stopped and had chosen this method to get his own way.

Al sped along the motorway, pushing the speed limit. It wasn't very far, but the traffic was heavy, so it was almost an hour before he turned into a gravelled driveway and pulled up in front of an imposing Georgian house.

'Come on,' Al ordered shortly, pushing open his own door and getting quickly out.

As Kenzie followed him she looked up at the sky and shivered. It was still daylight, but the sky was even greyer now, the clouds ominously dark. 'It looks as if there's going to be a storm,' she said uneasily.

Al's face immediately blazed with anger. 'How the hell can you talk about the weather at a time like this? Doesn't anything matter to you?'

'Yes, of course, but...'

Without waiting to hear, Al grabbed her hand and ran with her up the steps to the door. As they reached it, it was thrown open by a middle-aged woman who, at any other time, would be described as elegant, but now looked completely distracted.

'Alaric! Thank goodness you're here.' And she burst into sobs on Al's shoulder.

Al put his arms round his mother and led her back inside. Kenzie hesitated on the doorstep, but he hadn't forgotten her. Looking at her over his mother's head, his eyes cold and contemptuous, Al dared her to follow him in. With an inner sigh, Kenzie did so.

Another woman had come out into the hall. She drew Al and his mother into a room off to the left, a big sitting-room with windows opening on to the garden. 'Bring her in here, Alaric. I'll get her a brandy.'

'Oh, no, please. So stupid of me. I'm all right, really.'

But both Al and the other woman helped his mother to a chair and insisted on giving her a drink.

'Oh, dear.' Mrs Ellison managed a weak laugh. 'Drinking this early in the day—you'll turn me into an alcoholic.'

She was being very brave now, probably ashamed at having given way in the relief of seeing her son. Kenzie instinctively knew that she was a nice woman, someone she would have liked given half the chance. It was as this thought came into her mind that Mrs Ellison glanced past Al and saw her. The older woman froze for a moment, then clutched at Al's arm.

'Alaric! That girl... Surely that's—that's...'

'Yes. It's the Mackenzie woman. I've brought her here so that she can see just how much misery and suffering she's caused.'

'Oh, my dear boy! I know you meant well, but you shouldn't have done that.'

Kenzie whole-heartedly agreed with her; she felt completely out of place here, especially in the clothes she was wearing. The *couture* dress, high heels and auburn wig were intended as her costume for a sophisticated party, not for the drama that was being enacted here.

'I take it that there's been no news of Clive?' Al was saying.

'No, none.' It was the other woman who spoke. 'The grounds have all been searched, of course, but now John has taken the car to go and look for him, and the gardener and another two men have gone on foot into the forest, but it's such a big area to cover. John said they were all to come back at eight, and if there's no sign of him by then we'll just have to call in the police.'

'That's fair enough.' Al glanced at his watch. 'Which way have they gone?'

'I'll show you.' They walked over to the window so that the woman could point out the area.

Kenzie was still standing in the doorway; Al's mother turned her head and stared at her as if she were some strange, rather frightening monster. 'Why have you done this to us?' she said on a trembling note. 'Why are you raking it all up again?'

Al turned at the sound of her voice and came quickly over. 'It's all right, Mother; I'll explain everything later. Now I'm going out to help look for Clive.'

'You're not leaving *her* here?' his mother asked in alarm.

Al gave Kenzie an icy glare. 'No. I'm taking her with me.' He gave his mother a hug. 'Try not to worry, Ma.' He didn't attempt to tell her that everything would be all right, to give her any hopes that might be dashed, Kenzie noted. Straightening up, he walked into the hall. Kenzie followed and he closed the door. 'This way.'

She expected him to go out to the car, but he took her to a back hall where there was a row of pegs with waxed jackets, scarves, overcoats and macs hanging from them. Underneath were several pairs of boots.

'Here, these should fit you.' Al thrust a pair of green wellies and a waxed jacket at her.

'Oh, no. I'm not——'

In a sudden movement, Al grabbed her shoulders. 'You heard what I said in there; I'm taking you with me. So put them on.' Their eyes met, his murderously angry, her own wary. 'And take that damn stupid wig off!'

There was no arguing with him while he was this mad, Kenzie realised, and when he reached up a hand to tear the wig from her head she quickly put her arm up to stop him. 'No, I'll do it.'

She shook her own hair loose and left the wig hanging from a peg like some Red Indian's trophy. Outside the wind had risen and great black scudding clouds formed an ominous sky.

She hung back. 'I'll wait in the car.'

'No, you don't, you little coward. You're coming with me.'

'But I'll only slow you down. You can go much faster on your own,' she protested.

'I've seen you striding out; you can keep up.' Clad like her in boots and waterproof jacket, Al set off across the garden and through an orchard, leaving the grounds by a small gate that opened on to a high-banked lane. He walked at a fast pace, but when she lagged behind, hoping that he would go on without her, he turned, took hold of her wrist, and made her keep pace with him.

'Why are you making me go with you?'

'If there's anything to see, then I want you to see it,' he said harshly.

'There won't be,' Kenzie said shortly, made angry by being dragged along like some dog.

Al came to an abrupt stop, making her bump into him. 'What do you mean?'

'Ellison will be all right; I know it. He isn't the type to do any harm to himself, only to others.'

'You callous little bitch! He could be lying out there with his head blown in.'

'I bet he isn't!'

Fury leapt into his eyes, and for a moment she thought that he was going to hit her, but Al swung away and strode on, pulling her with him. They left the lane by a footpath that led into the forest. It wasn't a man-made forest of row upon row of conifers; this was natural woodland with mostly deciduous trees, lush ferns growing at their feet, and here and there fallen trees that were gradually disintegrating and becoming part of the forest floor. It would have been beautiful with the sun shining through the trees and the birds singing, but today the woods were ominously still, the birds safely tucked away in their nests.

Kenzie hung back again as they entered it. 'There's going to be a storm. I—I don't like storms.'

'Tough! You'll just have to get wet.'

'It's not that. I . . .' But Al was striding on.

He had no need to drag her now; Kenzie lengthened her stride and kept closer to him. She kept glancing up at the sky, her eyes afraid. That was how she came to miss her footing, stumbling over a tree root to pitch down over the edge of a ridge and fall about eight feet, ending up against the trunk of a tree.

'Are you all right?' Al scrambled down to join her.

'Yes.' She stood up and brushed dirt off her hands. Luckily the thick jacket had saved her from all but a few scratches on her knees. Looking round, Kenzie saw that she had fallen into a large, deep hollow in the ground, possibly once the bed of a large pond long ago dried out but leaving the ground lush with undergrowth.

'I'll give you a hand back up.'

Al went to climb up, but Kenzie said, 'Wait. Look.' She pointed to a distinct trail of bent and trodden-down grass where someone had walked through the dell towards an outcrop of rocks on the far side.

'It's probably only a deer trail,' Al remarked, but he began to follow it, Kenzie close behind him.

The rocks were very overgrown with bracken and would have been almost impossible to see from above, but when they rounded a tree they could see there was a fissure big enough for a large animal—or a man—to go through. The trail led straight to it.

'Stay here. I'll take a look,' Al ordered, his tone sharp with the awareness of what he might find.

He had to stoop and turn sideways to get through the hole, but it was easy for Kenzie when she followed him into the darkness beyond.

Al gave an exasperated sigh. 'I thought I told you...'

But Kenzie had moved further in, no longer obliterating the light, and they both saw the figure sitting on the ground, his back against the wall, eyes closed and head drooping. A gun lay on the floor beside him.

'It's Clive! Dear God, he's done it. He's dead! We're too late.' Al turned to Kenzie, his face grey with shock. 'How the hell am I going to tell my mother? This is your doing! You little...'

But Kenzie pushed past him to peer at Ellison in the dim light. She reached for his pulse, and a strange snuffling noise broke from his mouth. Straightening up,

Kenzie gave Al a derisive look. 'The dead don't usually snore,' she pointed out acidly.

'He's asleep? Are you sure?' Al leaned closer, then gave a small exclamation and picked up a hip-flask from the floor, its top open. He smelt and shook it. 'Whisky. And it's empty. Perhaps he drank it to give himself the courage to pull the trigger.'

'Or to while away the time while he waited for someone to find him,' Kenzie said coldly. She picked up a piece of paper from the floor. 'This looks like a piece of a chocolate wrapper. Perhaps he thought he might also need some sustenance while he worked up the courage to kill himself.'

His face grim, Al pushed past her. 'Get out of the way.' Reaching into Ellison's pocket, he pulled out the rest of the wrapper, then another chocolate bar. Taking hold of his stepfather's shoulder, he roughly shook him awake.

'What? Who is it? Alaric?' Ellison blinked, yawned, and put up a hand to rub his eyes. 'Where ... Oh!' His face paled as he saw where he was.

'Yes,' Al said savagely. 'You fell asleep and we've found you in your hole. Which wasn't what you meant to happen, was it? *Was it*?' He shouted the last words at him and shook him again. 'What did you intend—to be found wandering in the woods, still determined to kill yourself? While all the time my mother is growing ever more frantic with worry! You scheming bastard! I ought to knock your head off.'

He looked as if he would, too, his clenched fist held in front of the other man's face. Ellison cringed back against the wall, his eyes round with fear. 'I only wanted you to give up the enquiry. I can't take any more.'

He'd said the right thing. Al hesitated, but the anger was still in his face as he said, 'After today I'm beginning to wonder why. Did you pay Johnston to make that confession? Answer me, damn you! Did you pay him?'

But although Ellison was frightened he was too wily to implicate himself, and refused to answer, just went whinging on about his nerves, and his bad heart, until Al pushed him away in disgust.

'He isn't going to commit himself. Let's get out of here,' Kenzie said urgently. 'Your mother will want to know he's OK.'

Al nodded, but his face was still very grim as he said, 'Come on, you,' and pulled Ellison to his feet.

The older man picked up the gun and followed them outside. Kenzie scrambled out of the hollow and on to more open ground, then lifted her head to look anxiously at the almost black sky. Behind her she heard Ellison say, 'Who's that girl?' then give an exclamation. 'It's the Mackenzie woman! That bitch! The meddling, officious——'

Al gave a shout and she swung round to see that Ellison had levelled the gun at her! Kenzie stood in frozen horror, too shocked to move, but Al swiftly stepped in front of her, shielding her with his own body. 'Don't be damn stupid!' he said to Ellison, his voice sharp.

'Get out of the way! I'm going to kill the interfering bitch,' Ellison shouted, trying to step round him.

Shock giving way to fear, Kenzie quickly got close up behind Al, her heart thumping.

'And go to prison for the rest of your life—for her?' Al said forcefully.

'It would be worth it!'

'Then you're going to have to kill me, too.' There was a silence as Ellison took this in, then Al held out his hand. 'Give me the gun, Clive. Enough damage has been done.' But he didn't say who had done it.

Ellison hesitated for what seemed to Kenzie an eternally long moment as she waited behind Al, unable to see, but picturing their faces in her imagination. Then he said, 'Oh, all right. Here, take it. I'm tired.'

He handed the gun over; Al broke it and put the cartridges in his pocket. 'Let's get back to the house,' he said shortly. He turned and looked at Kenzie. 'I'm sorry.'

She shrugged. 'He's half drunk.' Quickly she turned away, and didn't see the look of surprised admiration in Al's eyes.

Going back the way they'd come, Kenzie set a fast pace, wanting to get back before the storm broke, but Ellison couldn't walk so fast and slowed Al down. 'Go slower, Kenzie,' he called. 'He can't keep up.'

'No, come on. We've got to hurry.'

She set off again, Al and Ellison some way behind, Al having to help him along. Kenzie tried to keep to more open ground, but there were too many trees all around. Hurrying along, she saw with thankfulness that the trees were becoming sparse; they must be almost at the edge of the forest. Her eyes kept going up to the sky, but, even so, the first lightning flash took her by surprise and she cried out in fright.

'What is it?' Al called out to her, but his voice was almost drowned in the clap of thunder that followed, a great, ear-splitting roll that seemed to rock the earth. The sky now was completely black and suddenly rain began to fall, as if thrown down from the sky in fierce, spiteful shafts by angry gods.

'Come on!' Kenzie ran out into the open then turned to scream the words at Al.

He tried to hurry, but Ellison hung back and pulled Al towards a big oak tree to take shelter beneath its outspread branches.

'No! Get away from the trees.'

Another great flash of lightning crackled across the sky, its jagged forks serpents' tongues of fire, lighting up the sky like brightest day. Kenzie threw herself on the ground and put her hands over her head, trying to make herself one with the grass and the soil. Thunder came, tremendous in noise and bombast, deafening, terrifying. Kenzie didn't want to get up, didn't even want to open her eyes, but she made herself do it. Al and Ellison were still under the tree. Al was trying to pull him away, but he had the gun in one hand and Ellison was pulling him back and shouting at him.

'Oh, hell!' Kenzie moaned. Pushing herself to her feet, she ran back to them, tearing along through the pouring rain. Coming up to them, she grabbed Ellison's other arm. 'Drop the gun. Leave it,' she yelled at Al. 'Just get him away from the trees.'

Al hesitated, then dropped the gun on the ground. Putting one arm round Ellison's back, and with Kenzie pulling his other arm, they ran the older man between them towards the open ground. As they did so a third explosion of lightning lit the sky. This time it was directly above them. Kenzie gave a desperate cry of terror as she forced herself to run on and not throw herself down again. Suddenly there was the most terrible noise behind them.

'My God! Look,' Al shouted.

Attracted by the metal gun, the lightning had hit the tree, and, mighty oak though it was, had almost riven it in two. Flames ran along the branches but were immediately quelled into hissing quiet by the torrential rain, and the gun lay in a scarcely recognisable twisted heap of molten metal.

It was too much for Kenzie; she screamed and went down on her knees, her head clenched in her hands, her arms tight over her ears. Letting go of Ellison, Al dropped to his knees beside her, putting his arms round her protectively and holding her close against him. 'It's all right,' he comforted. 'We're safe here.' But Kenzie was sobbing with fright, her body shaking with it, and hardly heard him.

The storm travelled on, passed them, driven by the wind and its own force. Soon it was just a rumble in the distance; the rain stopped and the skies began to clear.

'Kenzie?' Al's voice was gentle. 'The storm's over. Look.' Putting a hand under her chin, he lifted her head.

'No, no.' She tried to bury herself in his shoulder again, but he was insistent and wouldn't let her.

'Listen—no thunder. It's stopped.'

She couldn't avoid listening, then slowly, reluctantly, she opened her eyes. 'Oh, thank heavens! Thank heavens.'

'Not a very apt tribute in the circumstances,' Al said with a grin. He looked into her white, tear-stained face. 'You're really afraid of storms, aren't you?'

'I have reason to be,' Kenzie said bitterly. And, because she was still demoralised, confided, 'My parents were killed by lightning when they were sheltering under a tree.'

Al stared at her. 'And yet you came back and helped me to get Ellison away. If you hadn't we would surely have been killed. Kenzie, I——'

But she had recovered enough to realise he was her enemy and his arm was round her. Quickly she got to her feet, wiping her face with her hand. She looked round. 'Ellison has gone. No, there he is, running towards the lane.'

'We'd better go after him,' Al said grimly, as he, too, stood up. 'I want to talk to my mother before he does.'

'You go ahead, then. I—I'll catch you up.'

He gave her an uncertain glance. 'You're sure?'

'Yes. Go on; you'll have to run.'

'You can find your way?'

'Yes,' Kenzie said steadily. 'I know my way from here.'

Al frowned, hesitated as he looked after Ellison, then said, 'I'll see you later, then. Kenzie—we have a lot to talk about.' He paused, waiting for her to agree, but Kenzie said nothing, and he had to turn and go after Ellison.

Kenzie watched him, then took a handkerchief from her small clutch-bag which she had shoved into the pocket of the jacket, and wiped her face, pushing the wet hair from her forehead. Briskly then she walked to the lane, but, instead of going in the direction of the house, turned the other way and strode along, her face set and determined.

Kenzie stood at the side of the set, waiting for the introductory music to be played. But it was early yet, another five minutes before *Saints or Sinners* was due to start. It was a programme that was to have been the first of the new series, but now was also to be the very last one. She glanced across at the producer. He was standing a few feet away, which was hardly surprising; it had taken quite a while before he would even speak

to her again after she'd told him she wouldn't do any
more programmes after this.

It had been quite a titanic struggle to get her own way.
He had waved her contract at her and threatened to sue,
told her she would never work again. But Kenzie had
been adamant, and eventually he had had to give in.
Then she'd told him that she intended to discard the wig.
For a few alarming moments she had thought that he
was going to have either hysterics or a heart attack; he'd
grown very red in the face, then had thrown down the
papers he had been holding and stridden to the door.
'Do what you want! Ruin your whole image!' he shouted
melodramatically. 'I wash my hands of you.'

Surprisingly, in the last few days he seemed to have
come to terms with her decision and had taken his usual
close interest in the programme that was about to be
filmed. Not a terribly interesting one—there was to be
no live interview tonight; instead they were to show extracts from the previous programmes—but it would
satisfy the viewers and it was a traditional way for a
series to end. And it would also give Kenzie the opportunity she needed to make the apology that Al had demanded, not in such full form, but it would be an
apology, nevertheless.

She glanced towards the audience, who had been in
their seats for some time. The warm-up man was standing
in front of them, doing his usual patter, helping them
to relax so that they would react to the programme.
Seeing them made Kenzie remember the audience for the
last programme she had done at the end of the previous
series. Although she hadn't known it, Al had been among
them. Afterwards he had asked to see her, but she had
refused until it had been too late. If she'd seen him then
he wouldn't have gone to the lengths he had; he would

never have gone after her to Portugal—and they would
certainly never have become lovers.

Kenzie pushed that thought out of her mind, just as
she had pushed Al out of her life ever since the day of
the storm. When he'd left her she had walked to the
nearest telephone box and ordered a taxi which took her
back to her hotel in London. It hadn't taken her long
to pack and she had immediately checked out and rented
a flat instead. The doorman there and at the television
centre had been given instructions not to let Al in, and
her secretary told not to put his calls through. He had
tried to phone, she knew, and when he wasn't successful
had sent several letters. Recognising his writing, Kenzie
had shredded them unopened, along with his faxed messages asking her to contact him.

If the letters had contained the detailed explanation
and apology Al had demanded she read out tonight, then
it was just too bad. He would get his apology, but it
would be on her terms, not his. And there was no danger
of him being in the audience tonight; the security men
had been told to be especially alert and they had checked
every ticket holder.

The music started, the logo came up, and Kenzie
walked on to the set, a set that tonight held only one
chair. The audience gave a gasp when they saw her dark
hair and noticed that she was wearing a far more
feminine outfit than she normally wore for the programme. A ripple of comment went through them before
Kenzie could speak.

'Good evening, ladies and gentlemen. As you can
see——' she gestured at the single chair '—tonight is
going to be somewhat different. And I'm afraid I have
to tell you that this is the very last programme in the
series.' This provoked another gasp of astonishment, and

she made an empty-handed gesture. 'There are still a great many saints we can interview, but unfortunately the sinners have got wise to us and even their vanity isn't enough to stop them being too scared to risk exposure. So tonight we're going to go back over the series and show you some extracts that I'm sure you're going to enjoy seeing again.'

She paused, then lowered her head to look straight into the camera. 'But first I want to give an apology to a number of people who, up until recently, I haven't given much thought to. During the series we have exposed some twenty or so sinners, and have felt fully justified in doing so because we knew that it would stop them from doing more harm now and in the future. I wish to stress at this point that we have never exposed anyone unless that person has taken on new responsibilities in which they should have revealed their past but have not. We did not go out looking for them; in every case a member of the public was suspicious and appealed to us for help. And we checked and double-checked the evidence before we invited them on the programme. They could have refused; they weren't forced to appear.' She gave a small, rather cynical smile. 'But sinners are often very vain.'

The audience gave an appreciative laugh, as she knew they would, but then Kenzie continued. 'Often these people had kept their past a secret, not only from employers, but also from their neighbours, and in some cases their families. To have a member of your family or someone you love exposed on this programme must come as a very great shock. People whose only crime was to be close to a sinner have been ostracised because of it, their lives ruined. I have seen this for myself—and it is those people to whom I wish to apologise. In the hope of saving people from misery we have inadvertently caused misery ourselves. I am sincerely sorry. And that is another reason why this is to be the last programme.'

Kenzie stood for a moment, to pause before going into the extracts, and was totally unprepared for the sudden storm of applause that came from the audience. It must be a cue-card, she thought, and looked over to the floor manager's position, but he wasn't even there. The audience were applauding of their own accord. She smiled, held up her hand for quiet, and went to speak, but before she could do so heard someone walk on to the set. She glanced quickly round—only to stare in stunned disbelief as Al walked up to stand beside her.

Oh, God! she thought. 'He isn't satisfied with the apology; he wants his ounce of flesh. He's going to tell them all about his mother and Clive Ellison. She looked wildly round for the producer, the security men. How the hell had he managed to get into the studio? Why weren't they rushing forwards to drag him off the set? There should be enough of them even if he put up a fight. But she didn't want him to put up a fight; he might be hurt, put in prison. Her mind a chaos of jumbled thoughts, Kenzie went to swing away, to call to the floor manager, but Al reached out and stopped her.

To her even greater amazement, he then looked towards the cameras, smiled, and said quite calmly, 'Kenzie was right when she said that tonight was going to be different, but wrong when she said there were no more saints or sinners. There is one.' He gave the audience one of his most charming grins. 'My name is Alaric Rogan, and tonight I'm going to interview the very last "saint" or "sinner".'

Kenzie couldn't believe her own senses. Why don't they cut? she thought frenziedly. Why don't they turn the cameras away—*do anything*? But nobody moved and, keeping a firm hold of her wrist, Al led her to the chair and put her into it. As soon as he let go she tried to get up again, but he stopped her with a hand on her shoulder. Then, at last, the floor manager came on the set—but all he did was bring on another chair for Al to sit in!

She stared, open-mouthed, as Al again turned to the cameras. 'As you can see, we've taken Kenzie completely by surprise. And, as I'm sure you've guessed, *she* is the person I'm going to interview tonight.'

There was a gasp of astonishment from the audience and an even bigger one from Kenzie. She stood up. 'No! I won't do it. I——'

'Are you afraid?' Al asked her, his blue eyes quizzical. 'Too afraid to go through what you have put so many other people through?'

She looked at Al, then at the producer. He, like the rest of the crew, was standing with a big grin on his face. So he knew; they all knew. Somehow Al had coerced them into letting him do this—by bribery, probably—although the producer would do anything for a good programme, and exposing her would probably seem like a very good joke, especially when he was so mad with her. Kenzie's chin came up and she sat back in the chair, her legs crossed, apparently at ease, but her hands clutching the chair arms tightly. Bleakly she wondered if Al had given the Press the video and photographs as well, whether she was to be exposed in every form of the media—and exposed in more ways than one, she thought with cynical irony.

Seeing that she had accepted the challenge, Al sat down, then said, 'Kenzie, I understand you have a villa in Portugal?'

Oh, no, she thought with bitter misery, not that. It took all her acting experience, everything she knew, to keep her face expressionless and her voice cool as she answered, 'Yes, I do.'

'But you aren't able to spend all that much time there yourself. So who uses it when you're not there?'

She blinked and frowned, not expecting that. With a small shrug, she said, 'I occasionally lend it to people.'

'Not only lend it,' Al said. 'You also pay the air fares and provide spending money and all the food for a great many people who haven't been able to afford a holiday for themselves. People like overworked doctors, those who have been ill, young families going mad in bed-and-breakfast accommodation. And now I understand that you have *given* the villa to a charity so that orphaned children in the Third World and war-torn countries can holiday there, and even included the present caretakers to look after the place.'

Kenzie stared at him. 'How did you...?' She stopped, not knowing what to think. Was he treating her as she had treated so many of the sinners, spelling out the outwardly good things they were involved in, and then going in for the kill? She tried to get out of the chair, throwing a beseeching look at the producer. 'No. Please.'

But Al said, 'Sorry, Kenzie; it's your turn for the hot seat. You've just got to sit back and take it—just like all the other people before you.'

That ought to have been a threat, but there was no menace in Al's voice; if anything, he was looking amused. Slowly she sank back, but gave him a look of complete bafflement. 'Why? Why *you*?'

But Al ignored that, instead saying, 'It has come to my attention that once a week, for the last two years, you have been staying out all night—working ten-hour night-shifts for the Friends in Need! Through working for them, and also through this programme, you have helped needy people who have been brought to your attention, always generously—and always anonymously. One child in particular has reason to be grateful to you; his mother rang the Friends in Need for someone to talk to because she was so desperate. Her child was ill and needed an operation—one that could only be performed in America, and would cost thousands of pounds, which she had no hope of raising. Within a week all the arrangements had been made and that child was on its way to America.'

Again there was spontaneous applause from the audience, more prolonged this time.

When it died down, Al went on, 'You have been asked to front several charities so that your name can be used, but, having talked with the directors of those charities, I've been told that no way are you just a figure-head; you not only appear when asked, but also do a lot of behind-the-scenes work for them, even down to putting letters in envelopes.' He smiled and turned towards the cameras. 'There is one charity in particular to which Kenzie gives a great deal of time. This is to give help and comfort to people, especially youngsters, whose parents have died or been killed. She does this because...' He broke off as Kenzie suddenly started forward, an urgent appeal in her eyes. Al gave a brief, reassuring nod, then went on, 'Because she has the ability to identify with them.'

Getting to his feet, Al went to the centre of the set. 'There is a lot more I could tell you, ladies and gentlemen. How, when the music students who have small flats in the same house as Kenzie were threatened with eviction because they made too much noise practising, she bought the house and let them stay on. And how Kenzie doesn't forget old friends, finding work for several fellow actors.' He glanced round and grinned as he saw the stupefied look on Kenzie's face as she wondered how on earth he'd found out that she'd got Richard an audition for a new soap, a part he'd got and by now wasn't too proud to accept. 'As I said, I could go on, but I think I've managed to embarrass Kenzie enough. She'll probably kill me if I say anything else. So instead we have a surprise for her. There are a great many people that she has never met but who very much want to meet *her*. The first of these is a young man who is back from America and in the best of health.'

There was a fanfare of music and a little boy came on to the set, his huge grin almost hidden behind the basket of flowers he carried that was nearly as big as himself.

Kenzie gave a cry of astonished pleasure and knelt down on the floor to take the flowers and smile and talk to the child, her face filled with delight. But she'd only talked to him for a couple of minutes when his parents came on, and then people who'd been her guests at the villa, and then others she'd helped, until the set became full of people. Winston and her other Friends in Need colleagues were there, and even all the staff from her office, laughing at the way they'd kept the secret.

The closing music came on and Al said to the audience, and the millions of viewers, 'It has given me very great personal pleasure tonight to present your very last saint, Donna Mackenzie.'

He held out his hand to her, and she moved away from the others to come slowly forward.

'And I hope that it makes amends, my love,' he said softly.

She stared at him, for once in her life lost for words. He gave her a quizzical, almost strained look, eyebrows raised and she realised that he was still holding out his hand to her. To put her hand in his would be to accept this unexpected and most unorthodox apology, and it would also accept his two last words—with all that they implied. With a sudden, brilliant smile, Kenzie placed her hand in his. Al's grip immediately tightened, as if he was afraid she would change her mind, and he grinned back, his eyes alight with happiness.

The audience roared out their applause, the music grew to its crescendo, and Kenzie turned to the cameras. 'Goodbye. Goodbye.' She waved, but only with one hand, because Al still had a tight grip of the other.

He held it again, some hours later, after the great party he had thrown for her and all the guests—so great that it had gone on too long for his liking, and he had been impatient to get her to himself. But now they were alone at last, back in her old flat. They had kicked off their shoes and were sitting on the bed, a bottle of champagne to hand.

'How on earth did you get the producer to agree to changing the programme?' Kenzie asked him.

'When I put it to him he couldn't resist. He could see straight away what great television it would make.'

'But how did you find out all those things about me?' she demanded. 'They were supposed to be secret.'

'I run a bank; I can get hold of any information I want.' He grinned. 'And besides, I made friends with Babs; she told me an awful lot.'

'Did she, indeed?' Kenzie said indignantly. 'But how did you find out about the villa?'

'I'd written to Maria to thank her for her hospitality at the festival. She wrote back and told me.' Al smiled at her. 'There are a great many people who have reason to be grateful to you, my darling.'

Immediately she covered his mouth. 'I don't want to talk about that.' Lowering her hand, she looked at him gravely. 'What's happened to Clive Ellison?'

'He's gone. My mother threw him out, thank goodness. He'd lied to her from the start, and caused her enough heartache. She's getting a divorce and is looking better already now that she hasn't got him on her back.' He looked at her. 'He's caused us enough heartache, too. When I got him back to the house that day, after the storm, I made him admit that he had cheated the charity over the old people's home. And he also admitted that he'd given Johnston a large payment on the very day he made that sworn statement. Johnston was dying, all right, but he wanted the money to leave to his children.'

'Yes, I know. My researchers found that out.'

Al shook his head in disgust. 'It was all a tissue of lies. A cover-up. But Ellison was so plausible. My mother was completely taken in by him. And so was I, for that matter. He protested his innocence so volubly, showed me the statements, seemed so credible. And because I love my mother so much, I wanted to believe him. While all the time he was lying through his teeth,' he added bitterly.

'I don't think he instigated the cheating,' Kenzie remarked. 'I think it was Johnston. The trouble was that Clive Ellison had a rosy picture of himself getting a medal for all his good deeds. He took on too much charity and local government work and left the building of the old people's home to Johnston, who took advantage of it to line his own pocket. Then, when Ellison did find out, he was afraid to say anything in case he lost his reputation and his chance for a medal. So he stayed silent, until the place collapsed and he lost his reputation anyway.'

'I ought to have found that out for myself, though,' Al said, still feeling guilty. 'But when I got the message in Hong Kong that my mother had had a breakdown, and found out about Clive's attempted suicide... They were both so upset, my mother so ill. And everything lay at your door. I'm afraid I over-reacted, went overboard.' He drew her to him and kissed her temple. 'Can you ever forgive me, my darling?'

She laughed. 'I thought I already did—in front of several million people, too.'

'Good,' he said, in a way she remembered and loved. 'There is just one thing, though.'

Al had been about to kiss her neck, but he raised his head to give her an enquiring look. 'What's that?'

'Why did you rush away the day after we—we made love?'

'Isn't it obvious? I'd gone to Portugal with the sole intention of finding a way to get a hold over you. Then we met and I was immediately attracted. I was forever having to remind myself why I was there, make myself remember my poor mother. You surprised me at every turn, with your kindness, your modesty and lack of pretension. Sometimes I couldn't believe you were the same person. But I'd seen the video of your interview with Ellison, and I knew that, whatever you were in private, professionally you could be the she-devil they said you were. Even so, I didn't want to set up those cameras. But I knew I had to. I had to do it, then get out straight away, because I knew I was falling in love with you, and if I didn't act at once I wouldn't be able to go through with it.'

'But did you have to go so far—be so cruel?'

'I had gone out there hating you, but instead I found myself overwhelmingly attracted to you, more than to any other woman in my life. I *needed* to hate you, afterwards, for making me fall in love with you; that's why I had to utterly humiliate you. I wanted to make you grovel so that I'd feel justified in hating you. But you stood up to me with pride, took everything I threw at you with such courage... Oh, God, Kenzie, I'm sorry.'

They were both silent for a few moments, remembering, then Kenzie said, 'Would you really have given the video and those photographs to the Press?'

Al gave a short laugh and shook his head. 'Not in a million years. I just had to come on strong in the hope that you'd be too scared to call my bluff. But you weren't, of course.'

'I made the apology.'

'*And* gave up the series. You didn't have to do that.'

'Oh, yes, I think so. I wouldn't have been happy going on with it—not any more.'

Taking her glass from her, Al began to kiss her neck. 'Well, I'm not altogether sorry, because now we'll be able to go away on a long honeymoon.'

'Mmm.' She squirmed deliciously. 'Where?'

'How about your villa in Portugal?' Kenzie opened her mouth to remind him that she'd given it away, but saw the devilish look in his eyes. 'I bought it back, gave them a larger one.'

'Oh, Al!' Throwing her arms round his neck, Kenzie kissed him ardently. The kiss grew deeper and he began to unbutton her dress, but she moved a little apart and said, 'Al? The video and those photographs; you have destroyed them, haven't you?'

'I destroyed the copy of the video, yes.'

'What about the original?'

He shook his head. 'No way. How many men get to relive the most wonderful night of their life? And as for the photographs...' His face broke into a huge grin. 'You remember that one of your back-view in the little apron, bending over the table? I'm going to have that one blown up to life-size and framed.'

Kenzie burst into laughter. 'What on earth for?'

'So that I can give it a little pat every time I go past.' His eyes changed, darkened. 'But that's only when I haven't got the real thing around, of course.' And he drew her into his arms.

IT'S FREE! IT'S FUN! ENTER THE

☆ "Hooray for ☆ Hollywood" ☆

SWEEPSTAKES!

We're giving away prizes to celebrate the screening of four new romance movies on CBS TV this fall! Look for the movies on four Sunday afternoons in October. And be sure to return your Official Entry Coupons to try for a fabulous vacation in Hollywood!

☆ If you're the Grand Prize winner we'll fly you and your companion to Los Angeles for a 7-day/6-night vacation you'll never forget!

☆ You'll stay at the luxurious Regent Beverly Wilshire Hotel,* a prime location for celebrity spotting!

☆ You'll have time to visit Universal Studios,* stroll the Hollywood Walk of Fame, check out celebrities' footprints at Mann's Chinese Theater, ride a trolley to see the homes of the stars, and more!

☆ The prize includes a rental car for 7 days and $1,000.00 pocket money!

Someone's going to win this fabulous prize, and it might just be you! Remember, the more times you enter, the better your chances of winning!

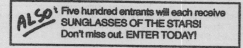

ALSO† Five hundred entrants will each receive SUNGLASSES OF THE STARS! Don't miss out. ENTER TODAY!

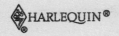 HARLEQUIN® 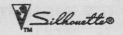 Silhouette®

The movie event of the season can be the reading event of the year!

Lights... The lights go on in October when CBS presents Harlequin/Silhouette Sunday Matinee Movies. These four movies are based on bestselling Harlequin and Silhouette novels.

Camera... As the cameras roll, be the first to read the original novels the movies are based on!

Action... Through this offer, you can have these books sent directly to you! Just fill in the order form below and you could be reading the books...before the movie!

48288-4	Treacherous Beauties by Cheryl Emerson		
		$3.99 U.S./$4.50 CAN.	☐
83305-9	Fantasy Man by Sharon Green		
		$3.99 U.S./$4.50 CAN.	☐
48289-2	A Change of Place by Tracy Sinclair		
		$3.99 U.S./$4.50CAN.	☐
83306-7	Another Woman by Margot Dalton		
		$3.99 U.S./$4.50 CAN.	☐

TOTAL AMOUNT	$
POSTAGE & HANDLING	$
($1.00 for one book, 50¢ for each additional)	
APPLICABLE TAXES*	$ _____
TOTAL PAYABLE	$ _____
(check or money order—please do not send cash)	

To order, complete this form and send it, along with a check or money order for the total above, payable to Harlequin Books, to: **In the U.S.:** 3010 Walden Avenue, P.O. Box 9047, Buffalo, NY 14269-9047; **In Canada:** P.O. Box 613, Fort Erie, Ontario, L2A 5X3.

Name: _____

Address: _____ City: _____

State/Prov.: _____ Zip/Postal Code: _____

*New York residents remit applicable sales taxes.
  Canadian residents remit applicable GST and provincial taxes.

CBSPR

"HOORAY FOR HOLLYWOOD" SWEEPSTAKES

HERE'S HOW THE SWEEPSTAKES WORKS

OFFICIAL RULES — NO PURCHASE NECESSARY

To enter, complete an Official Entry Form or hand print on a 3" x 5" card the words "HOORAY FOR HOLLYWOOD", your name and address and mail your entry in the pre-addressed envelope (if provided) or to: "Hooray for Hollywood" Sweepstakes, P.O. Box 9076, Buffalo, NY 14269-9076 or "Hooray for Hollywood" Sweepstakes, P.O. Box 637, Fort Erie, Ontario L2A 5X3. Entries must be sent via First Class Mail and be received no later than 12/31/94. No liability is assumed for lost, late or misdirected mail.

Winners will be selected in random drawings to be conducted no later than January 31, 1995 from all eligible entries received.

Grand Prize: A 7-day/6-night trip for 2 to Los Angeles, CA including round trip air transportation from commercial airport nearest winner's residence, accommodations at the Regent Beverly Wilshire Hotel, free rental car, and $1,000 spending money. (Approximate prize value which will vary dependent upon winner's residence: $5,400.00 U.S.); 500 Second Prizes: A pair of "Hollywood Star" sunglasses (prize value: $9.95 U.S. each). Winner selection is under the supervision of D.L. Blair, Inc., an independent judging organization, whose decisions are final. Grand Prize travelers must sign and return a release of liability prior to traveling. Trip must be taken by 2/1/96 and is subject to airline schedules and accommodations availability.

Sweepstakes offer is open to residents of the U.S. (except Puerto Rico) and Canada who are 18 years of age or older, except employees and immediate family members of Harlequin Enterprises, Ltd., its affiliates, subsidiaries, and all agencies, entities or persons connected with the use, marketing or conduct of this sweepstakes. All federal, state, provincial, municipal and local laws apply. Offer void wherever prohibited by law. Taxes and/or duties are the sole responsibility of the winners. Any litigation within the province of Quebec respecting the conduct and awarding of prizes may be submitted to the Regie des loteries et courses du Quebec. All prizes will be awarded; winners will be notified by mail. No substitution of prizes are permitted. Odds of winning are dependent upon the number of eligible entries received.

Potential grand prize winner must sign and return an Affidavit of Eligibility within 30 days of notification. In the event of non-compliance within this time period, prize may be awarded to an alternate winner. Prize notification returned as undeliverable may result in the awarding of prize to an alternate winner. By acceptance of their prize, winners consent to use of their names, photographs, or likenesses for purpose of advertising, trade and promotion on behalf of Harlequin Enterprises, Ltd., without further compensation unless prohibited by law. A Canadian winner must correctly answer an arithmetical skill-testing question in order to be awarded the prize.

For a list of winners (available after 2/28/95), send a separate stamped, self-addressed envelope to: Hooray for Hollywood Sweepstakes 3252 Winners, P.O. Box 4200, Blair, NE 68009.

CBSRLS

OFFICIAL ENTRY COUPON

"Hooray for Hollywood"
SWEEPSTAKES!

Yes, I'd love to win the Grand Prize — a vacation in Hollywood —
or one of 500 pairs of "sunglasses of the stars"! Please enter me
in the sweepstakes!

This entry must be received by December 31, 1994.
Winners will be notified by January 31, 1995.

Name _____

Address _____ Apt. _____

City _____

State/Prov. _____ Zip/Postal Code _____

Daytime phone number _____
(area code)

Mail all entries to: Hooray for Hollywood Sweepstakes,
P.O. Box 9076, Buffalo, NY 14269-9076.
In Canada, mail to: Hooray for Hollywood Sweepstakes,
P.O. Box 637, Fort Erie, ON L2A 5X3.

KCH

OFFICIAL ENTRY COUPON

"Hooray for Hollywood"
SWEEPSTAKES!

Yes, I'd love to win the Grand Prize — a vacation in Hollywood —
or one of 500 pairs of "sunglasses of the stars"! Please enter me
in the sweepstakes!

This entry must be received by December 31, 1994.
Winners will be notified by January 31, 1995.

Name _____

Address _____ Apt. _____

City _____

State/Prov. _____ Zip/Postal Code _____

Daytime phone number _____
(area code)

Mail all entries to: Hooray for Hollywood Sweepstakes,
P.O. Box 9076, Buffalo, NY 14269-9076.
In Canada, mail to: Hooray for Hollywood Sweepstakes,
P.O. Box 637, Fort Erie, ON L2A 5X3.

KCH